"It's our turn to swing."

Cougar tugged on her hand.

She saw the wide plank seat on the huge, dark, hulking tree and realized what kind of swinging he had in mind.

He caught her at the waist with a long shepherd's crook of an arm. "Come sit on my lap and let's ride double. This is a two-passenger swing. They don't make 'em like this anymore."

She took a rope in each hand, kicked off her shoes and lowered herself onto his lap.

He took his hat off and tossed it in the grass, pushed off the ground with his booted feet just as she stretched her legs out behind his back. They were flying low, chasing evening shadows with bright smiles.

She leaned back on the upswing. "This is crazy!"

His first kiss came mid-flight....

Dear Reader,

Nothing stirs this air force brat quite like a marching band and a formation of men and women in uniform parading before me. Military service goes way back on my side of the family, and many of my forebears rest at Arlington National Cemetery. And I married a man in uniform. My husband shipped out thirty days after our wedding. His people, the Lakota Sioux, have, like most American Indians, proudly served in the U.S. military in great numbers for well over a hundred years.

Cougar—"just Cougar"—is such a man. He's served gallantly, and he has the scars to prove it. He carries most of them on the inside. Little does he know that he wears his heart on his sleeve, where it's easily stolen by a boy with special needs and a woman with love to give.

Once again, those magnificent wild horses from the Double D Sanctuary have a way of bringing people together.

All my best,

Kathleen Eagle

One Brave Cowboy

KATHLEEN EAGLE

First published in Great Britain 2013
by Mills & Boon, an imprint of Harlequin (UK) Limited.
Large Print edition 2013
Harlequin (UK) Limited,
Eton House, 18-24 Paradise Road,
Richmond, Surrey TW9 1SR

© Kathleen Eagle 2011

ISBN: 978 0 263 23758 0

Harlequin (UK) policy is to use papers that are natural,
renewable and recyclable products and made from
wood grown in sustainable forests. The logging
and manufacturing process conform to the legal
environmental regulations of the country of origin.

Printed and bound in Great Britain
by CPI Antony Rowe, Chippenham, Wiltshire

KATHLEEN EAGLE

published her first book, a Romance Writers of America Golden Heart Award winner, in 1984. Since then, she has published more than forty books, including historical and contemporary, series and single titles, earning her nearly every award in the industry. Her books have consistently appeared on regional and national bestseller lists, including the *USA TODAY* list and the *New York Times* extended bestseller list.

Kathleen lives in Minnesota with her husband, who is Lakota Sioux. They have three grown children and three lively grandchildren.

Remembering Daddy
Honoring the American soldier

Chapter One

The driver of the black pickup was himself driven, fixed on the hulking two-story white house at the end of the road. It was an old house in need of a coat of paint with a brand new, freshly painted sign affixed to the porch railing.

Office

Double D Wild Horse Sanctuary

It was the kind of incongruence that automatically drew his eye and raised the hackles he'd been working hard to tame. He was back in the States, for God's sake. *South Dakota*. Land of the granite chiefs and home of the original braves. Just because something was a little off in a place that seemed too quiet didn't mean Cougar needed to crouch and prepare to pounce. He was there on a tip from a fellow soldier. About the only people he trusted these days were guys he'd served with, and Sergeant Mary Tutan was one of the most standup "guys" he knew.

She couldn't pull rank on him anymore, but she'd tracked him down, got him on the phone and talked like she could. *Get your ass in gear, soldier! Go check out the wild horse training competition my friend Sally Drexler is running. It's just what the VA docs ordered.*

She'd corrected herself—Sally *Night Horse*—and explained that Sally had married an Indian guy. Did he know Hank Night Horse? How about Logan Wolf Track?

As if Indian country was that damn small.

Cougar wasn't interested in the sergeant's social life, but the mention of horses got his attention. *Training competition* and *cash prize* sounded pretty attractive, too. He'd been away from horses too long. The one he could see loping across the pasture a good half mile away made him smile. Nice bay with a big spotted colt in tow. He could almost smell their earthy sweat on the hot South Dakota wind blowing through the pickup cab.

His nose welcomed horse sweat, buffalo grass and the clay dust kicked up by the oversize tires on his "tricked out" ride, compliments of his brother, Eddie. He could have done without the tires. Could have done without any of the surprises he'd come home to, but he didn't want to do without his brother, and Eddie would have pouted indefinitely if Cougar had said anything about how many miles his brother had racked up on the vehicle in Cougar's absence.

The house looked pretty quiet for the "headquarters" of what was billed as the biggest privately maintained wild animal reserve in the Dakotas. Cougar didn't care how big it was as long as it was legitimate. He'd been down too many dead-end roads lately. The end of this one seemed pretty dead as far as human activity was concerned, but one by one the horses were silently materializing, rising from the ebb and flow of tall grass. They kept their distance, but they were watchful, aware of everything that moved.

As was Cougar. His instinct for self-preservation wasn't quite as sharp as the horses', but it surpassed that of any man, woman or...

...child.

Cougar hit the brake. He saw nothing, heard nothing, but eyes and ears were limited. Cougar knew things. Men and women were on their own, but kids were like foals. Always vulnerable. They gave off signals, and Cougar was a gut-level receptor. Which was a damn good thing. If it hadn't been for his gut, he would have done nothing.

And if it hadn't been for the red baseball cap, he would have thought he was going crazy again, and he might have slid his boot back over the accelerator. But the red cap saved both kid and driver.

And the goat.

Cougar's pulse pounded behind his staring eyeballs. The goat took off, and a small hand stretched out, barely visible beyond a desert camo armored fender.

Don't stop for anything, sergeant. That kid's coming for us. You slow down, he takes us out. Do. Not. Stop.

Cougar closed his eyes, took a breath, shifted into reverse as he took a look back, gunned the engine, and nearly jackknifed his trailer. When he turned, there was no goat. He saw a light-haired kid in blue jeans, stretched out on his belly. He saw the front end of his black pickup. He saw a red and white barn, sparsely graveled road and South Dakota sod. He secured the pickup and threw the door open simultaneously. His boots hit the ground just as the kid pushed himself up on hands and knees. He looked up at Cougar, eyes filled with terror, but no tears.

And he was up. *Thank you, Jesus.*

Cougar's shadow fell across the boy like a blanket dropped from a top bunk. His own knees wouldn't bend. "You okay?"

The boy stared at him.

"I didn't see you," Cougar said, willing the boy to stand on his own, to *be able to* get up all the way. "Are you hurt?"

The boy stretched out his arm, pointed across the road and smiled. Cougar swung his head around and saw a gray cat.

"Was that it?" He looked down at the boy. "A damn cat? For a second I thought I'd…"

His legs went jittery on him, and his knee cracked as he squatted, butt to boot heels. "Jesus," he whispered as he braced his elbow on his knees and dropped his head into his hand. His heart was battering his ribs. He couldn't bring himself to look the kid in the eye quite yet. Might scare him worse. Might scare them both worse.

A small hand lit like a little bird on his shoulder. He twitched beneath it, but he held himself together. He saw the red cap out of the corner of his eye, felt the wind lift his hair, smelled the grass, heard the pickup purring at his back. His own vehicle, not the Army's. He held on to the here and now, lifted his head and gave the boy a quick once-over, every part of him but his eyes. He couldn't trust himself to look the boy in the eye. He wasn't strong enough yet.

"That was close, wasn't it? Scared the... livin'..."

Not a word from the boy.

Cougar took the risk of patting the hand on his shoulder. It was okay. His hand was steady. "But you're all right, huh? No harm done?"

No response. Kid was either scared speechless, or he was deaf.

Or blind. One eye, anyway. The other eye didn't move. Cougar looked him up and down again, but the only sign of blood was a skinned knee peeking through a stained hole in his jeans.

Wordlessly the boy turned tail and sped away like a fish running up against a glass wall. Cougar stood slowly, pushing off on his thighs with less than steady hands, lifting his gaze from the soles of the boy's pumping tennis shoes, down the road to the finish line.

The barn's side door flew open, and there was Mama. She was all sound and flurry. "Mark!"

Get set, go! Cougar heard within his head, where his pounding pulse kept pace with retreating feet. He got back into his pickup and let the tires crawl the rest of the way, passing up the house for the barn, where the woman—small, slight, certainly pretty and pretty certainly upset—would be somebody to talk to. The options—all but one—weren't exactly jumping out at him.

He parked, drew a long, deep breath on the reminder that he hadn't killed anybody today and then blew it out slowly, again thanking any higher power that might be listening. The doc's slow, deep breathing trick seemed to be working.

"Is the boy all right?" Cougar called out as he flung the pickup door shut.

The woman held the boy's face in her hands, checking for damage. Cougar watched her long, lush ponytail bob and weave as she fussed over her charge. It swung shoulder to shoulder as she turned big, bright, beautiful brown eyes on Cougar. "What happened?"

For the sake of those wondrous eyes he wished he had an answer. "Whatever he told you." He took a step, testing his welcome. "I'm still not sure."

"He hasn't told me anything. He doesn't speak."

Cougar looked down at the boy, who appeared to be taking his measure. "So you weren't holding out on me. But you took off before I got around to saying I'm…" He offered his hand. "I'm sorry. I didn't see you."

"What *happened?*" the woman insisted.

"I'd say he came out of nowhere, but that would sound like an excuse. All I know is that I slammed on the brakes, and…" He shook his head. "Then I saw his cap, then a hand and I thought I'd, uh…*hit*—" he glanced at the boy, and his stomach knotted "—somebody."

"You stopped *before* you saw anything?"

"Yeah. Well, I…" He owed it to her straight, just the way he remembered it. "I had a feeling. It's hard to explain. I guess I was admiring the scenery." He adjusted his new brown Stetson, stirred some gravel beneath his shifting boots. "I didn't see him. Didn't hit the horn, nothing."

"I was just getting some…" She gestured toward the door she'd left open. "Oh, God, I wasn't paying attention. I let him slip…" She gave her head a quick shake. "*I* slipped. For a minute. *More than a minute.*" She pulled the boy's head to her body. The top of it fit nicely between her breasts. He gave her a quick hug and then ducked under her arms and backed away, leaving her empty arms still reaching for him. "Oh, Markie-B, I thought you were playing with the kittens."

"I guess the mama got away. He was chasing her." Cougar's gaze connected with the boy's. "Right, Mark? You were just trying to bring Mama Cat back to her babies."

"Was it close?" the woman asked, almost inaudibly.

"He must've tripped. He was face-in-the-dirt. Blew the knee out of his jeans." He turned to the woman. "He can't hear, either?"

She shook her head. "As far as we know."

"Don't they have tests for that?" *You just crossed the line, Cougar.*

"Yes, of course. Tests. All kinds of tests." She offered him her hand. "I'm Celia Banyon. My son, Mark, is a mystery. We really don't know what's going on."

"Yeah, it was close." Either the truth or her touch made him weaken inside. He glanced away. "Really close."

"I'm… He looks…" She cleared her throat, stepped back, and her hand slid away. "Are you here to see Sally?"

That's right. He was on a mission that had nothing to do with a stray kid.

"I'm here about the training contest. The name's Cougar."

"First? Last?"

"Always." She gave him a puzzled look, and he took a shot at smiling. "Just Cougar. One name is enough." He glanced at the house. "Is she here?"

"Nope, it's just me and Mark holding down the fort today. Everyone else is either out in the field or taking care of business. You're a trainer?"

"I've trained my own horses, yeah. I heard about this wild horse contest from a friend, so I thought I'd have a look for myself, see if I can qualify."

"Mustang Sally's Wild Horse Makeover

Competition. I'm not actually involved. We're volunteers with the sanctuary. Aren't we, Mark?" She touched the boy's shoulder, and he looked up at her. "We help Sally with the horses, don't we?" Then turning her attention back to Cougar, she shaded her eyes with her hand. "Sally and her husband had an appointment. Everyone else is working. I could get you an information packet from the office." She glanced at the boy. "We need to go in and take care of your knee anyway, don't we?"

Mark was staring at Cougar, who felt obliged to honor the eye contact since the boy seemed to be a few senses short of a full house.

"Where was he?" Celia asked. "He couldn't've been far away. Right? He was right here with me, and then…"

"He's pretty quick on his feet."

"I know." She sighed. "Boy, do I know."

"I'll come back later." Cougar stepped back, giving the woman plenty of space for worries that were no longer his business. The boy was unharmed.

"If you'd like to leave Sally your number…"

"I'll call her later. Think I'll head back over to Sinte and hang out for a while."

"I'll let Sally know." When he stepped back, she quickly added, "Where are you from?"

"Wyoming. Wind River country."

"Did you make a special trip?"

"Up until I met up with Mark it was pretty ordinary."

"I meant…" She reconsidered, and then she nodded, reached for the boy and drew him under her wing. "Next time…"

"Yeah." He gave a wink when he caught Mark's eye. "We'll be careful. We'll watch out for each other."

Down the road, Cougar ran across the gray cat. She was sitting exactly where he'd last seen her, as though she was waiting to be picked up. He stopped and did exactly that. The cat didn't object, not even when he slid his hand around her belly. He could feel her swollen teats. The gooseneck trailer he was towing complicated his U-turn, but he wasn't about to back down the road. He knew a thing or two about blind spots.

Celia appeared in the doorway, shaded her eyes and watched him warily. Probably thought he'd been casing the place and come back to cause mayhem. Couldn't blame her.

"I found the cat," he called out as he

alighted, holding the animal to his chest. "Thought it might be a comfort."

"Thank you." She didn't reach for the cat, and he didn't offer it. She looked a little ashen. Delayed shock, maybe. They just looked at each other while he stood there like an overgrown kid, rubbing the cat behind her ears.

"She would have come back," Celia said as she led the way into the barn.

The cat started purring. He liked the feel of it. "I'm like the boy. Don't want her getting too far away from her litter."

"Mark's playing with them. I don't think he realizes. I haven't done a good job of impressing it on him that he has to…he can't just…"

Cougar squatted beside the boy and released the cat into the newspaper-lined box, to the delight of her squirming, mewling kittens.

"Oh, look how welcome Mama is," Celia said.

Cougar watched the kittens latch on to Mama for lunch. Mark was busy making sure all seven were hooked up. He didn't seem to realize that disaster had zoomed in so close that its sickening taste still filled Cougar's mouth. Maybe the boy had already filed the lesson away, and it would serve him down the road. Cougar wished he could do the same—a wish he probably shared with the kid's mom. He turned, looking for confirmation, a little eye contact with her big, magnetic brown eyes, but she wasn't there anymore. Not the hovering kind, apparently.

But how did she know Cougar wasn't some kind of a whack job? She'd already told him he had the two of them pretty much all to himself. He'd drop a word of caution if he were the interfering kind of a...

He heard soft mewling—the human variety—coming though an open door to a dark room. He assured himself that the boy was thoroughly occupied before he stepped close to the door.

"Celia?" Her name rolled off his tongue as though he'd been saying it for years.

She drew a hiccough-y breath. "I'm...okay."

She's okay. Walk away.

"Doesn't sound like it."

"I just don't want him to see me," she whispered desperately.

Cougar stepped through the door. It was a tack room, and the woman stood tucked among the bridles. Small and slim as she was, she might have been one of them.

"How close was it, really?" she asked, her voice reedy.

"Close."

"You couldn't see him, but you stopped?"

"That's right." He didn't quite know what to do with himself now that he'd crossed his own line. He'd just met the woman, and he felt like he was looking at her naked. He took a leather headstall in hand and hung on, steadying himself for a bumpy ride. "Some people have eyes in the back of their head. I have something inside my head. It picks up where the eyes and ears leave off. *Sometimes*. Not... not always."

"Whatever it is, I need some."

He gave a dry chuckle. "It doesn't always turn out this good."

"It did this time. Mark's in his own world,

and I'm on the outside, trying to look in. I blink, and he gets away from me." She drew a quavering breath. "But he's not hurt. What am I blubbering about?"

"I've still got the shakes, too. We know what could have happened. Mark doesn't, so he doesn't need to worry too much right now. We can do that for him."

"He *does* know what could have happened. Somewhere in the back of his mind he knows better than we do." She swallowed so loudly Cougar could taste her tears. "He had a terrible accident. Lost an eye."

"Car accident?"

"No. It happened…" She shut herself down. He had all the details he was getting right now. "This isn't the first time I blinked."

"Won't be the last. You got another pair of eyes in your family?"

"Mark's father and I are divorced." She paused, shifting gears. "I want what you have. A mother's instincts aren't enough with a child like Mark."

"Ordinarily I'd say *take mine,* but I'm glad I had it goin' on today."

"Me, too." She took a swipe at each eye with the back of her wrist as she emerged from her little harbor. "Just Cougar?"

"It's all I need. Pretty big name."

"It's a great name." He took half a step back as she edged past him. A singular moment had passed. "You know, the winner of the training contest gets twenty thousand dollars."

"Yeah, that's what Sergeant Tutan said."

He followed her through the tack room door. "Mary Tutan. She's the one who told me about the competition."

"Oh, yes, Mary," she said, her voice brightening. "She just got married."

"I stopped in and met her husband before I came here. She's..."

"...back in Texas."

"Says she's put in for discharge. Kinda surprised me." Seeing the boy with the kittens made him smile. "Sergeant Tutan had *lifer* written all over her. She's a damn good soldier. Uncle Sam will miss her, but she's served well."

She took his measure with a look. "You, too?"

"I've been out for two months now. Officially." Which was like saying her son had

had an accident. There was a lot more to it, but nobody wanted to go there. "Tell Sally I'll be at Logan's place. I'll check back in with her." He reached down and touched Mark's shoulder. "You've got a nice family there." The boy offered up a little calico. Cougar rubbed the top of its head with his forefinger and nodded. "They're too young to leave their mama."

"Maybe we'll see you when you come back for your horse," Celia said. "You'll get to choose."

"If Mark's around, maybe he could help me with that." He still had the boy's attention, maybe even some awareness of what he was saying. Cougar felt some connection. Close calls could have that effect. He'd experienced enough of them to know that. "I'll bet you know the mustangs around here pretty well. I could use your advice."

"He'd like that," Celia said. "Thank you. I…" She laid her hand on his arm. Against his will he turned, took her eyes up on their offer of a clear view into her heart. "Thank you."

He couldn't wait to get out the door. He couldn't handle that kind of gratitude. It wasn't about anything he'd done. It was about not doing the unthinkable. At best it was about an accident that hadn't happened, and he needed to put some distance between his image of what might have been and the faces in the image.

At the same time he wanted to hang around, which was pretty damned surprising. And it was about as uncomfortable as a new pair of boots.

* * *

Logan Wolf Track lived in a log house just outside the town of Sinte, where he served as a tribal councilman for his Lakota people. Cougar's mother had been Lakota, but he was enrolled with the Shoshone, his father's people. Cougar hadn't met Logan until he'd knocked on the Wolf Track door the previous night. Sergeant Mary Tutan Wolf Track was the person they had in common. A white woman, strangely enough.

Or maybe it wasn't that strange. Indian country was more open these days than ever before, what with the casinos and educational programs that opened up opportunities for people on both sides of what had long been an unchallenged fence. But before these changes and beyond Indian country, there had been the military. Cougar's people had been serving in ever-increasing numbers for generations.

Cougar had been an army police officer—an MP—and Mary had been a dog handler. She'd served as a trainer—most recently in Afghanistan—and as far as Cougar was concerned she was the best trainer in uniform. She'd paid him a visit in the hospital in Kandahar, and she'd written to him after he was transferred stateside. More recently, they'd spoken by phone. Their mutual interest in training animals had given her something cheerful to talk about, and when Mary had talked up the wild horse training competition, she had his full attention. She'd planted an idea that had pulled him out of the seclusion he'd sought after his release from a VA hospital.

Cougar was glad to see Logan's pickup parked in his driveway. It wasn't home—Cougar towed his house around with him these days—but Logan Wolf Track was the kind of guy who made you feel at home. Fellow Indian, fellow cowboy, husband of a fellow soldier. Logan opened the door before Cougar's knuckles hit the wood.

"Did you get signed up?" Logan asked as he handed Cougar a welcoming cup of coffee.

"Not yet." Cougar settled in the kitchen chair Logan offered with a gesture. "The boss was out."

"Nobody around?" He said it like such a thing never happened.

"There was a woman. A volunteer, she said.

And her kid." Cougar took a sip of kick-ass and cut-to-the-chase coffee. He closed his eyes and drew a deep breath. "I almost ran over the kid."

Logan let the quiet take over, leaving Cougar to take his time, sort though the images. They were jumpy, like an old silent movie, until he came to the woman. Her face was clear in his mind, and her voice poured over the images like slow dance music.

"He's okay," Cougar said. "Came out of nowhere, but I hit the brakes in time. Scared the hell out of me, and I think *I* scared the hell out of his mom. The kid…" He shook his head. "Hell, he didn't seem to notice. Can't talk, can't hear and he's half blind. I didn't see him." Another sip of coffee fortified him. "Damn, that was close."

Logan put a plate of frybread on the table and took a seat across from his guest. "Your pickup sits up pretty high."

Cougar nodded. "I gotta get rid of those monster tires. My little brother had the truck while I was gone, and he thought he was doing me a favor tricking it out like that. Coming home present, you know?"

"How do they ride?"

"Like saddling up a plow horse. Somehow I gotta tell Eddie the monster truck days are behind me."

"That's hard. A gift is a gift."

"And the monster truck was a kid's dream." Cougar lifted his cup. "Good coffee. Tastes like Green Beans. Honor first, coffee second," he recited, paying tribute to one of the few things he missed about being deployed in the Middle East.

Logan smiled. "You and Mary were in the same outfit?"

"No, but she worked pretty closely with us. She's a real specialist. I'm the guy nobody invites to the party."

"But when the party turns ugly, it's the guy with MP on his sleeve who kicks ass in a good way."

"That's what we're all about. I've kicked a lot of ass." He helped himself to a piece of frybread. "You've been over there?"

"Gulf War." Logan claimed a piece of frybread and tore it in half. "I was a kid when I went over there. Came back desperate to find some kind of normal. I found myself a hot woman and married up. She cooled off real fast. Took off and left me with her two boys. Who became my two boys." He took a bite out of the chewy deep-fried bread. "Did Mary tell you we're gonna have a baby?"

"Already?"

"Hell, yeah. You know what else? Normal's the name of a town somewhere. Who needs Normal when you've got Sinte, South Dakota? Or…Wyoming, right? Where in Wyoming? You probably—"

"I probably didn't say. Right now it's wherever I park my outfit." He nodded toward the front door. "Room to haul two horses and sleep two people."

"What else does a guy need?" Logan asked with a grin.

"Not much." Cougar gazed out the patio door and past the deck toward Logan's corrals and pole barn. It wasn't a fancy setup, but it was trim and orderly. "My brother and I have some land west of Fort Washakie. We own a quarter section, and we leased some grazing land, but he gave up the lease while I was gone." He lifted a shoulder. "Can't blame him. I was gone."

"Were you running cattle?"

"I had horses. Eddie had to sell them." But that wasn't what he wanted to think about right now. He turned back to his new friend. "You know the people over at the Double D pretty well?"

"I know Sally. She and Mary have been friends a long time. Hell of a woman, that Sally Night Horse. She has multiple sclerosis, but she doesn't let it slow her down much." Logan offered a knowing look. "She has a lot of volunteers coming in to help. What's the name of the woman you met?"

"Celia Banyon. The boy's name is Mark."

"Oh, sure. Celia's a teacher." Logan smiled. "Pretty little thing."

"Pretty enough." Logan's smile was slightly irritating, but Cougar caught himself half smiling, too.

"Careful," Logan said. "You crack your face, you're gonna feel it."

Cougar laughed. "Ouch. Damn, that smarts."

"It looks good on you. Like you said, no harm done. Shake it off, cowboy." Logan warmed up Cougar's coffee with a refill. "What kind of horse are you looking for?"

"A war pony. One that can go all day without complaining."

"You do know it's a contest."

"Mary said you can train the horse for anything you want."

"You have to turn out a useful horse. Not much call for war ponies these days."

"That's what *I'm* calling for. A war pony prospect." Cougar leaned back in his chair and stretched his legs under the table. "I did some endurance racing before I enlisted. Mustangs and Arabs are the best mounts for endurance, far as I'm concerned."

"That's how you'd prove your horse?"

"If they're pretty open on what you can train the horse for, I don't see why not. Endurance is a good sport. Good for the horse, great for the rider. From what I've read, it's even more popular than it was back when I tried it out. You think I can get approved to train a war pony?"

"I think you'd round out Sally's contestant collection pretty nicely." Logan grinned. "Especially now that I'm out of it."

"She needs an Indian replacement?"

"Indian *cowboy.*" Logan chuckled. "Talk about your dying breeds, huh? Cowboys are scarce enough, but us *Indian* cowboys…"

"Why'd you take yourself out?"

"The horses will be auctioned off after the thing is over, and my wife and I…" He smiled, clearly pleased with the words. "We decided Adobe was worth more to us than winning the competition, so we adopted him and took him out of the running."

"Sweet. The horse is out of the running. The owner's off the market."

"*Both* owners."

"Sergeant Tutan deserves the best." Cougar

glanced out the patio door again, taking in Logan's setup. "You've got a round pen out there. How do you like it?"

"When you get your horse, you come try it out. I wouldn't be without one."

"They weren't expecting me at the Double D," Cougar admitted. "I told them I was coming, but I didn't exactly say when. Sunrise this morning, I didn't think about it too much. Felt like a good time to take a drive."

"And now you're here," Logan said. "So take your time. Stay here tonight, and I'll head over there with you tomorrow. I never miss a chance to go looking at horses."

"I just need a place to park."

"Plenty of parking space, but there's also a spare room." Logan indicated the hallway with a jerk of his chin. "It's yours if you want it."

Cougar wanted peace and privacy. He needed to build a new life, and he would start with what he loved most.

Horses.

Chapter Two

Cougar spent the night in his trailer. The bed was comfortable—great memory foam mattress one of his fellow patients at the VA had raved about until Cougar had promised to get himself one if the guy would shut up about it—and all the basic necessities were covered. The best part was the solitude. Privacy had been hard enough to come by in the army, but hospitals were worse yet. Not only did you have people around every minute of every endless day and night, but you had them poking at your body and digging into your mind.

The trailer had been another of Eddie's homecoming surprises. *Got a great deal on it for you.* Eddie had used the money he'd gotten for their horses to buy his brother a horse trailer. It sounded like a story Cougar had read in English class back in the good ol' days, only in the story it wasn't the same person selling the two things that went together. Cougar would have taken his kid brother's head off if he hadn't actually been a little touched by the whole thing. They'd been partners, but the trailer was in Cougar's name. And in the end it was a relief to know that he could still be touched in the heart, what with it being general knowledge that he was touched in the head. So who was he to accuse "Eddie Machete" of being a madman?

Logan had offered Cougar the use of his man-size shower, and he planned to take him up on it, but not without knocking on the door with a few groceries in hand for breakfast. After honoring sunrise with a song, he un-hitched the trailer, drove into the little town of Sinte, parked in front of the Jack and Jill and waited for the doors to open.

The cashier gave him the once-over when he unloaded bacon, eggs and orange juice next to her register. He read the whole two-second small-town ritual in her eyes. Nope, she didn't know him.

"Anything else?" she asked tonelessly. Half a dozen smartass answers came to mind, but he opted for a simple negative.

With one arm he swept the grocery bag off the counter, thrusting his free hand into his key-carrying pocket as he turned to the door. Two big brown eyes stared up at him—one friendly, the other fake.

Cougar smiled. "Hey, Mark, how's it going this morning? Better than yesterday?"

"Yesterday?" A man about Cougar's size stepped in close behind the boy. His dark red goatee and mustache somehow humanized his pale, nearly colorless eyes. He laid a hand on Mark's shoulder, but his question was for Cougar. "What happened yesterday?"

So this is the ex-husband.

"We had a little run-in." Cougar winked at the boy as he scratched his own smooth jaw. "*Near* run-in. Mark was lookin' out for his cat, and I was looking at horses."

"Yeah?" With one hand the man adjusted his white baseball cap by the brim—the *Bread and Butter Bakery* emblem identified him apart from the woman and her boy—while he tightened the other around Mark's small shoulder and moved him two more steps into the store. "Where did all this happen?"

"The wild horse sanctuary. Are you...?"

"Mark's father."

Cougar drew a deep breath and offered a handshake. "The name's Cougar."

"What do you mean by *run-in?*" Handshake accepted, nothing offered in return. "Were you walking? Riding?"

"I was driving. I didn't see him. I drive a—"

"Where was his mother?"

"She was close by." Cougar eyed the hand on the boy's shoulder. He could feel the fingertips digging in. *Ease up, Mark's father.* "It was one of those things that happens so fast, nobody can really be—"

"In Mark's case, everyone has to be."

Man, those eyes are cold.

"I know. She told me. Guess that's why it scared me more than it scared him." He smiled at Mark, sending out *you and me, we're good* vibes. "But nobody got hurt, and we found the cat, and it was all good training."

"Training? She calls that *training?*"

"I call it good training." Cougar's keys chinked in his restive right hand. "Ever been in the army? If nobody gets killed, it's called good training."

"No, I haven't served in the military." Again he touched the brim of his cap. "But, you know…thanks for your service. Cougar, you said?"

"That's right."

"Could I get some contact information from you? I might want to get a few more details."

"About what?"

Not that it mattered. Cougar was all done with the pleasantries. He would have walked right through the guy and out the door if the boy hadn't been looking up at him the whole time, asking him for something. He didn't want to know what it was. He didn't have it to give.

"Mark is what they call *special needs*," Red Beard said slowly, as though he was using a technical term. "I'm his father, and I have rights. Not to mention a responsibility to make sure he's getting all the services and care he's got coming. You never know what you'll be able to use to back up your case."

"Case against who?"

"Not *against* anybody. *For* Mark. Proof that his needs are special."

"His mother knows how to reach me," Cougar said. He only had eyes for the boy as he stepped around the two. "Look both ways, Mark. I'll see you around."

Cougar smelled bacon. Damn, he loved that smell. He didn't miss much about being deployed in the Middle East, but food in camp was surprisingly good, and breakfast in "the sandbox" had been the best meal of the day. Unless you were manning an outpost, in which case every meal came with a side of sand.

Logan had gotten the jump on Cougar's

plan to prepare breakfast. He stowed most of his purchases in the fridge, set the bread on the table—gave the plastic Bread and Butter Bakery bag a second look and decided he wasn't in the mood for toast—and helped himself to coffee.

"I ran into that kid I told you about over at the Jack and Jill. He was with his dad."

Logan turned from the stove and the bacon he was lifting from the pan and raised an eyebrow. "When you say *ran into*..."

"I was on foot." Cougar watched the grease drip from bacon to pan. "His mother said he lost his eye in an accident. You know anything about that?"

"Not much. Happened on some kind of construction site, the way I heard it. Before she came here to teach. Her ex-husband started showing up a few months ago." Logan turned the stove off. "About all I know for sure is she's a good teacher."

"He wanted to know how to get in touch with me in case he needed some kind of witness or something. I don't know what he was talking about. It was a close call, but the boy wasn't hurt." Cougar drew a deep breath and glanced out the patio door toward the buttes that buttressed the blue horizon. "I'm sure he wasn't hurt."

"His mom checked him over?"

"Skinned his knee, but that's..." The image of the boy pushing himself up to his hands and knees brought back the wrecking ball swing—*boom!* panic, *boom!* relief. Even now his heart was racing again. "He doesn't talk. He can't really say what's..."

"At that age, they get hurt, most kids let you know with everything they've got except the kind of words that make sense. You get blood, bellowing, slobber, maybe the silent treatment, but you don't get the story until you've already assessed the damage."

"They break easy," Cougar said quietly.

"After they're grown, you look back at all the close calls and you figure somebody besides you had to be lookin' out for them." Logan handed Cougar a plate. "Go to the head of the line."

Cougar followed orders. Logan added finishing touches to Cougar's meal—the toast he didn't want and the coffee he couldn't get enough of—playing host or dad, Cougar wasn't sure which.

"My older son, Trace, he's a rodeo cowboy." Logan's plate joined Cougar's on the table. "He's broken a lot of bones riding rough stock. You gotta learn to bend, I tell him. Look at the trees that survive in the wind around here. We're survivors."

"Learn to bend," Cougar echoed.

He hadn't known Logan long, but he knew him pretty well. They'd worn some of the same boots—cowboy boots with riding heels, round-toed G.I. boots, worn-out high tops stashed under an Indian boarding school bed at night, beaded baby shoes. He knew the lessons, figured they'd both felt the same kind of pinching, done their share of resisting.

Considering all that, Cougar sipped his coffee and gave Logan a look over the rim of the cup.

"Pretty deep, huh?" Logan chuckled. "Spend

a few years in tribal politics, you learn how to command respect with a few well-placed words of wisdom. Everybody around the table says *Ohan,* so you know when it comes time to vote, you've gotten the ones who were on the fence to jump down on your side."

"So that's the way it works." Cougar set the cup down with exaggerated care. "Whatever passes for wisdom."

"It helps if it's true."

"I'm having a hard time with that lately. I thought it would all come clear to me as soon as I got back to the States, back home. It hasn't happened yet. Truth, justice and the American Way." Cougar's turn to chuckle. "What the hell is that?"

"Superman," Logan said with a smile. "I

heard he died. Never learned to bend, they said."

"Superheroes ain't what they used to be."

"No, but that cottonwood tree keeps right on spittin' seed into the wind." Logan nodded toward the glass door that opened onto a deck dappled by the scant shade of a young tree. "I don't know about you Shoshone, but the Lakota hold the cottonwood in high esteem. Adaptable as hell, that tree."

"Where I come from, we don't have many trees." Cougar finished off his eggs and stacked his utensils. "I could listen to you throw the bull all day long, Logan, but that won't get me into the wild horse training competition. Are we heading over to meet this Mustang Sally I've heard so much about, or not?"

Logan slid his chair back from the table. "My friend, let's go get you a horse."

Through the big barn doors Celia recognized the white panel truck when it was still the size of a Matchbox toy. It carried her heart's greatest delight and her mind's worst trouble. Part of her wanted it to slow down and take the Double D approach, and part of her wanted it to sail on past.

It turned.

It was too soon. She'd just seen her former husband last night when he'd come to get Mark for the weekend. He'd been civil enough, but that didn't make it any easier for her to be around him. Round two was bound to be uncivil. Either he'd invented some new bone of contention or devised another way to throw her off balance.

Or maybe something had come up and he was about to forego the rest of his time with Mark. No problem. No need to explain. *Just give my son back to me and say no more.*

Oh, if he would only say no more.

She finished dumping the contents of the wheelbarrow onto the manure pile, grabbed the handles and pointed the front wheel toward the barn. She didn't want to deal with Greg out in the open. Whenever there was a chance of an audience, he was *on*. His normal tone of voice was several notches higher than anyone else in the scene. And Greg loved a scene.

She wished she had time for a shower. Sure it was silly, but scent confidence always felt like a huge advantage. Stinker that he was, Greg rarely got his hands dirty.

Mark ran to his mother the moment he entered the barn. Celia got the message from his quick, strong hug—*I'd rather be with you*—and then he bolted for the cats' nest.

"We're on our way to Reptile Gardens," Greg announced. "We figured you'd be here, so we thought we'd stop in."

"This stop isn't on the way to Reptile Gardens." She pulled her rawhide work gloves off as she watched Mark claim a gray tiger in each hand and tuck them against his neck. She wanted to thank the mewling kittens and their patient mama for the bright laughter in her boy's eyes. "But Mark obviously needed to check on the kittens."

"The bakery changed my route. I've got

the Jack and Jill in Sinte now, and I made a special delivery there this morning. Ran into your new friend." Greg greeted her glance with a cold smile. "Calls himself Cougar?"

Celia tucked her work gloves into the back pockets of her jeans. She'd learned to ignore the inevitable preamble and go on about her business until Greg got to his point. He took fewer time-consuming detours that way.

"He said he almost ran into Mark yesterday. Could have killed him."

Not a direct quote, Celia decided. She hardly knew Cougar, but she was pretty sure he hadn't said that. Greg was baiting her. If she kept her mouth firmly closed, he would eventually go away. Maybe even without Mark if he could come up a glitch in his plan. News that the rattlesnakes had escaped from Reptile Gardens, maybe, or a tortoise quarantine.

"Why weren't you watching him?"

She hadn't braced herself for that one. It was a fair question, and it had been haunting her since the incident happened. Sarcasm evaporated. Who was she to criticize—even silently—when she'd failed so miserably?

"We were doing chores," she said quietly. "I thought he was—"

"*You thought.* See, that's your problem, Cecilia. You're always thinking. Meanwhile, he's on the move, many steps ahead of you. And who the hell knows what he's thinking?"

"He was playing with the cats."

"And what were you playing with? Huh? What were you playing with, Cecilia?" He grabbed her shoulder. "Or should I ask, *who?*"

Celia jerked away, but she took only one step back, fighting him off with a defiant stare. "You can ask about Mark. Obviously I wasn't playing with Mark. I was busy doing chores, and, yes, that's my—"

"It's not your job. Your job is that boy right—"

"Hey, Mark." Cougar strolled into the barn, flashing Celia a reassuring glance on his way to the cat's nursery. He squatted, touched Mark's shoulder and then a couple of kittens. "Are they all there? Did you take a head count?"

Mark pressed a kitten under Cougar's chin.

"Have you figured out how many boys and how many girls? I think the calico's a girl." He stood easily, confident in the silence his appearance had created. Without moving from the position he'd taken, he looked directly at Celia and offered a soft, intimate, "Hi."

"Hello." Silken calm slid over her. "I understand you two have met."

"Yeah, Mark introduced us." Cougar reached down to ruffle Mark's hair. The boy looked up and smiled. "I'm glad you're here. You can help me pick out a horse."

"My son and I have plans," Greg said. "I just stopped in to see what she had to say about what happened yesterday. So far—"

"I came over with Logan," Cougar told Celia. "Called first this time."

"That must be why the boys brought some of the horses in," she said.

He glanced at Greg as though he were an image on a TV show that nobody was watching. "Mark and I can go take a look if you two need to talk."

"Mark's with me." Greg moved to block Celia's view of everyone but him. "It's my weekend. Long as you're both here, maybe you can explain exactly how my son came to be out in the road and why nobody saw him until he was nose to nose with—"

"Because he's quick, and he's small," Cougar said. "Fate cut us a break. Be grateful."

"Don't tell me to be grateful." Greg pivoted and postured, hands on hips. "You don't know what we're dealing with here. But you will if I see any more evidence of emotional or psychological trauma."

Cougar chuckled. "You wanna sue me for something that didn't happen? What are you, a lawyer?"

"No, but I have one."

"Have at it, then. If I harmed this kid, I'll make sure—"

"He wasn't hurt," Celia insisted quietly. "He's fine, and he doesn't need to hear this."

"He can't hear, remember?" Greg's challenge swung from Celia to Cougar. "Doctors don't know why, but I do. It's because his mother left him to—"

"Greg, please. Let's not do this now. You know what's going to happen." She continued to speak in hushed tones while Mark went right on attending to the kittens. He was protecting himself in ways that she could not, but still she would do what she could. Maybe he *didn't* hear, but she believed he *could,* and when he was ready, he would. Meanwhile, he had keen senses, and she would not have him treated otherwise.

She moved past Greg and caught Mark's attention. "Let's go have a look at the mustangs."

"Hell with the mustangs," Greg bellowed. "Next thing I know, you'll have him wandering into the path of a pack of wild horses."

"They run in herds," Cougar said.

"Put the cats down, Mark." Greg grabbed Mark by the elbow and urged him to his feet. "We're going to Rapid City. We'll catch the snake show." His big hand swallowed the child's small one. "Like I said, I've got a lawyer. We're not done yet, Cecilia. Not by a long shot."

Cougar stood in the doorway and watched the boy tag along with his father, stretching his leash arm to its limit, dragging his toes in the dirt. He tamped down the urge to go after them, spring the ham-fisted trap and release the kid. Why wasn't there some kind of law against adults using kids to even a score? Maybe Cougar should make one. He'd gladly enforce it.

Come on, Mark's father, sue me.

"I'm sorry about that." Celia's soft voice drew him back into her company, where his anger began to cool. "I guess you could tell, we aren't exactly on friendly terms. I try not to say very much when he gets going like that. It's pointless to try to talk with him." She touched his arm. "Thank you for understanding."

"The guy already pissed me off once today, so the understanding part was easy. The hard part is watching Mark. He doesn't want to go."

"I know. But Greg has his new court order." She didn't sound too happy about it. "And his lawyer."

"It's none of my business," he reminded himself aloud. "Unless he wants it to be. In that case, bring it on."

"I hope not," she said with a sigh. "I'm tired of fighting. It's a distraction from figuring out what's best for Mark."

She sure sounded tired, and he felt bad about that, even though he was pretty sure whatever distraction he'd just caused hadn't been a bad thing. The truth was, he'd headed straight for the barn when he saw the bread delivery truck parked beside her little blue Chevy. He was in the habit of filing away the details of every vehicle he saw, where he saw it and whether it might blow up in his face down the road. After the conversation he'd had with Mark's father at the store, he'd done the math in his head—ex plus ex—and he'd chosen to butt in. It had taken him all of two minutes to develop a strong dislike for the man and become Celia's natural ally.

Which might have just added to her difficulties, dumbass. You don't know what's going on between these two people. When did you become lifeguard on this beach?

I saved a life yesterday, didn't I?

You came within an inch of ending one. Two, if you count yours.

"I don't have to pick out a horse today," Cougar said. "I can wait for Mark." Which was just a thought, in case anyone inside his head was listening.

"He loves them all. Whichever you choose, tell him you'll share. Come look." Celia gestured toward the far side of the barn. She led, and he followed.

They rounded the corner of the building, clambered up the tall rail fence and peered past a set of corrals. At least a dozen young horses milled about in a small pasture.

"They'll let you handle it any way you want. Run them all into the pens for a close look, turn out the ones that don't interest you, let you run your own test on those that do." She grabbed a piece of her sorrel-colored hair away from the wind and anchored it behind her ear. "It's fun to watch people make their selection. Sometimes they want the wildest one in the bunch. Other times you just know they're looking for one that looks like he's half asleep."

"I want one that's almost as smart as I am." He smiled at her. "But not quite."

"You said Logan was here? He's the one you should confer with. Have you read his book?"

"His book?"

"The one about how he trains horses," Celia said. "I can never remember titles, but it's the author's name that's important, and Logan Wolf Track is the real deal."

"The real deal, huh?" Cougar smiled. *So that's what a real deal looks like.* "I figured he was a good trainer. Didn't know he'd written a book, though."

"It's wonderful." Celia scrambled back down the fence, and Cougar jumped down after her. "I knew nothing about horses when I started volunteering here, and my friend, Ann, gave me Logan's book. Ann's Sally's sister. She's a teacher, too. We both teach at…" She waved at something that caught her eye behind his back. "He's over here!"

Cougar turned to find "the real deal" striding in his direction. Logan had parked in front of the house, and Cougar had promised to be along in a minute. No questions had been asked, no comments exchanged.

"Sally's waiting for you to fill out some papers, cowboy," Logan announced. "That's one woman you don't wanna keep waiting."

"Why not? She kept me waiting."

"That was yesterday. You keep her waiting today, you'll just be giving her time to think up something the sanctuary needs that nobody but you can provide." Logan clapped his hand on Cougar's shoulder. "Because you're just that special."

"What's your specialty?" Cougar asked Celia.

"Well, with a B.S. in education—Sally calls it a B.S. in BS-ing—we've found that I'm really good at distinguishing horse manure from boot polish."

The men looked at each other.

"Shinola?" Celia insisted. *"Boot polish?"*

Both men grinned. "Long story short, there was a time when she kept Sally waiting," Logan told Cougar.

Chapter Three

"I'm going with one of the Paints."

Cougar laid the form on Sally Night Horse's desk, most of the blanks, including the horse's ID number, finally filled in. He'd been leaning toward a bay that showed strong Spanish Mustang traits when Celia mentioned her son's attraction to the spotted horses, and the Medicine Hat gelding was the flashiest horse in the bunch.

"Good choice," Logan said. The two men exchanged looks—Logan's knowing, Cougar's *what the hell*. "Medicine Hats are sacred, and that one has classic war bonnet markings. Brown ears, little brown cap on his head. He'll show nicely."

"He'll cost you," Sally said.

Sally Drexler Night Horse had a way of filling a room with energy. She was the positive charge in the Double D's power grid, and her latest project had her chugging ahead full steam, even when she had to power up her wheelchair. Her office furniture gave her wide berth, and even though she wasn't tied to the chair, she wasn't apt to explain or deny it, either. Sally was in charge.

Clearly when she said *pay up,* a guy was expected to ask, "How much?"

"Your cowboy ass planted firmly on the line. Or the fence." Sally leaned to one side as though she were trying to get a look at the new applicant's backside. "In the saddle is good, too. We need eye candy for a documentary we're shooting."

"That Paint is pretty sweet." Cougar slid Logan a what's-up-with-this look. Logan chuckled.

"True, but you're the real bonbon. Put the two of you together..." She gave Cougar a sassy wink. "YouTube, here we come. And we'll be goin' viral."

"What do I have to do?" Cougar asked. He barely knew what YouTube was, which was already considerably more than he cared to know.

"The woman who's doing the video—Skyler Quinn—Logan's son, Trace, knows her pretty well. Right, Logan? The Double D is giving Match.com a run for their money lately. They hook you up on paper—or what passes for paper these days—but we make matches on the ground right here in horse heaven."

Logan laughed. "Skyler has Trace carrying her camera bags and loving every minute of it, all right."

"Sally's got talent," Sally quipped as she started scanning his application. "My husband, Hank, may be the singer in the family, but I know a thing or two about harmony. I know future soul mates when I see them."

She glanced over the edge of the paper and gave Cougar a loaded look with an enigmatic smile, which almost scared him. He was a private man, and right now she was holding some of the keys to his privacy on what had always passed for paper.

She went on reading, all innocence.

"Anyway, Skyler's out in Wyoming, and you're located in that beautiful, rugged, picturesque Wind River country. She'll love that." Sally flipped the application in Cougar's direction and pointed to a blank space. "You forgot to fill out this part. Location, location, location."

"I'm…kinda between locations."

"What does that mean?"

"Between a VA hospital and a home site in Shoshone country," he said impatiently.

The sergeant was supposed to have laid the groundwork here. If anybody had a problem with his recent history, he wasn't going to waste his time with any damned application. He'd been banged up a little and spent some time getting his head straight. He wasn't about to open up his medical records to get into a horse contest.

"But you ranch," Sally affirmed, adjusting her glasses as she took another look at what he was beginning to regard as his test paper.

"Did I say I'm ranching now?" The muscles in the back of his neck were threatening to knot up beneath the short hairs she was tugging on. "It doesn't say I'm still ranching. It says that's one of my qualifications. Right?"

In the time it took him to draw one of those cleansing breaths he'd been taught to practice, he was able to put everyone in the room out of his mind. It was just a piece of paper. "The answer to this question is ranching," he said calmly as he tapped the word with an instructive finger. "And this one…Wind River is where I'm from." He pushed the paper across the desk. "I put Sergeant Tutan down as a reference. Call her."

Sally turned the paper over. "Mary's your only reference?"

"Why didn't you put me down?" Logan asked him. "You're bringing the mustang over to my place."

"For a few days." Had he accidentally walked into a damn bank? He had half a mind to turn on his heel and walk out.

But his other half a mind remembered how far he'd have to walk to get to Sinte, where he'd left his roof and his ride—the two things he owned the keys to.

And the whole of his mind was set on taking

on that Paint gelding with the sweet brown "cap" pulled down over his ears. He had no idea what kind of endurance horse he'd make, but he didn't care about winning an endurance event. Running it from start to finish would do fine.

"I have a few acres. My brother and I turned our lease back and sold..." Be damned if he was going to stand here and recite his whole life story. He was glad Celia had gone back to the straightforward BS in the barn. "Look, I'm a civilian now, pretty much starting over."

Sally looked up with a genuine, no BS smile. "All we need is a location and a description of your facilities."

"Put down my place," Logan told her. "Are you coming to the celebration? You and Hank?"

"Wouldn't miss it. I hear Mary's coming home."

He turned to Cougar, grinning like a proud papa. "Don't say anything, but the celebration's for her. She just got a Commendation medal. Meritorious achievement. Did she tell you?"

"She didn't. That's some eagle feather to cap off a career."

"No kidding." Logan tapped Cougar's chest with the back of his hand. "You're coming, right? I need a color guard. You got your uniform packed away in that trailer of yours?"

"Your Lakota VFW will want to do the honors." Cougar had put his army green away for good. "But I'll be there. I'll step up to the microphone and pay tribute to her the Indian way."

"Put down my place," Logan urged Sally with the distinctively Indian version of a chin jerk.

"Cougar?" She wanted his word.

"Is that okay with you?" Cougar asked her.

"For now," she said. "But if anything changes..."

"I'm not gonna run off with your horse."

"I'm not worried about that, Cougar, and he's not my horse. I answer to the Bureau of Land Management, and you know how that goes. Red tape from here to Texas."

"Stand down, soldier," Logan said. "You're set for now. But you'll have to let Sally get some of that Shoshone country video footage she's lookin' for."

"*Footage* is boring," Sally said as she signed the form. She swung her chair and fed Cougar's commitment into her copier. She punched a button and followed up with a punch to the air. "Woo-hoo! Chalk up another Indian cowboy for the cause. Women are our target market, and they're not looking at your boots, boys."

Cougar had to laugh. He took damn good care of his boots. Spit and Shinola.

"You have a clean barn, Sally."

Cougar turned toward the voice. Celia stood in the office doorway, her shiny pink face framed by zigzagging tendrils of damp hair. The smudge on her jaw—some kind of boot polish, no doubt—called out for a friendly thumb to wipe it off. He rubbed his itchy palm on the outside seam of his jeans.

"Hey, Celia, thanks," Sally said. "You want some lunch?"

"I wondered if you wanted me to grain the horses they just brought in."

"Actually, I'm short-handed today, and there's something else I had in mind for you." Sally's dramatic pause drew Cougar's attention. "We really depend on our volunteers. They're mostly women, and I just hate piling so much on such slim shoulders."

Celia laughed. "Since when?"

"I know I don't thank you often enough, Celia, but I'm trying to do that right now," Sally deadpanned. "And in a meaningful way."

"I could help out while I'm here," Cougar said. "What do you want done?"

Sally hiked up the corners of her mouth, nodded and winked at him in a way that just didn't seem right for a married woman. "Put the man to work, Celia," she said.

Logan cleared his throat. "He rode over with me, and I have a—"

"Few hours to contribute? We're hauling bales and riding fence. Take your pick."

"I'll have to take door number three," Logan said. "The one marked Exit."

"But you're already committed," Sally said, cocking a finger at Cougar. "You'll be helping Celia, and she'll give you a ride back to Sinte." She glanced at Celia. "Is that okay with you?"

"What's the assignment?"

"Find out how six of our horses got into Tutan's pasture." Sally took off her glasses and waved them at Logan. "Your father-in-law—my damned neighbor—called the sheriff again. He doesn't believe in handling these things between neighbors."

"My father-in-law." Logan shook his head. "That's a real kicker."

"I sent a couple of the kids out, but they came up empty, said they couldn't find any fence down. I just want to make sure. If there's a hole in that fence, we'll get it fixed before Mary gets back." She made a smooth-sailing gesture. "Peace in the valley for Mary's sake. You think he'll show up at the celebration?"

"I doubt it. But she'll want to see her mother. She's only got three days this time." Logan lifted one shoulder. "Kinda sorry I planned this party now. Only three days."

"She's a short-timer," Sally said. "Pretty soon she'll be home for good. But I wouldn't put it past your *father-in-law* to run our stock into his pasture just to stir things up again. Which is fine by me—he cranks on his egg beater, I'll come back at him with my Mixmaster—but it's not fair to Mary."

"You can pick your wife, but not your in-laws. Listen, I'm all for mending fences, and I'd stay and help with it, but I've got a meeting," Logan told Cougar. He nodded at Sally. "Watch out for that one. She'll have you thanking her for letting you paint her fence."

Sally laughed. "If he's lucky he'll get to stretch some wire, but there's nothing out there to paint. I'll tell you what, though, I can't wait to paint this house. I don't care how many people try to horn in, I'm saving it all for myself." She wagged a finger at Cougar. "I might let you watch, but nobody's taking over on me."

"She'll get takers. You watch." Logan clapped a hand on Cougar's shoulder. "I gotta get goin'. I'll move the pickup so we can load up your mustang. I'll buy these two lunch, Sally. The Fence Rider's Special, on me."

"One volunteer sponsorship. That's going on your tab, Wolf Track."

"This woman knows how to rake in the donations," Logan told Cougar. "Better than a cable TV preacher." He gave Sally a two-fingered wave. "You oughta get yourself a show, Sally."

"People in love are so generous. Gotta strike while they're hot," Sally called out after Logan. Then she gave Celia the calculating eye. "A weekly TV show. How could we work that?"

Celia glanced at Cougar. She was smiling.

The horses weren't the Double D's only attraction for a woman packing some heavy cares. Cougar nodded, and her smile brightened even more.

"Oh! Speaking of hot irons," Sally said. She was checking her watch. "Hank should be pulling in any time now. He's been out shoeing horses for a team-roping club, and I'm not gonna let him cool off just yet." She rolled back from her desk, put her wheels in park and levered herself to her feet. "Just the thought makes me weak in the knees.

"So you guys get that horse loaded up and then help yourselves in the kitchen, will you? Pack up the Fence Rider's Special. Sandwiches, chips, water and a wire stretcher. Enjoy the ride." She winked at Cougar as she reached past him for her cane. "I know I will."

"Can't wait to meet her husband," Cougar whispered to Celia as they headed for the front door.

"Hank's a lovely man, and Sally's the rising tide that lifts all boats," Celia said. "She's unsinkable."

Ordinarily Cougar might have doubted the notion on the grounds that the person simply hadn't waded in deep enough, but Sally was far from ordinary. And Celia? If he drowned in the woman's eyes, it wouldn't be a bad way to go. As long as he didn't come bobbing back up to the surface and find himself in a mud puddle. He'd been there, and he wasn't going back.

He wasn't looking forward to loading a wild horse into a trailer, either, but Logan had him covered. No pushing, no pulling, no slapping. The closest thing Cougar had ever witnessed to Logan's display of patience was a dog training session with Staff Sergeant Mary Tutan, which led him to conclude that theirs was a match made in the kind of heaven where dogs and horses—the Lakota *sunka* and *sunka wakan*—dwelled side by side with human spirits. The notion made a pretty picture for Cougar to file among the good places he regularly sought for refuge when ugly thoughts crowded his damaged head.

"The Paint doesn't have a schedule," Logan said. "And we won't try to give him one. If our time runs out, we'll walk away and come back later."

Logan instructed Cougar to approach the trailer *beside* the horse, not ahead or behind, and to remember that horses were naturally claustrophobic. Cougar had no trouble sympathizing with that particular fear. It was one of several he'd brought home with him.

It turned out he'd chosen a horse that was compliant by nature, and Logan was able to drive away with him in time to make his meeting.

And then it was time to take a ride. Celia insisted on packing food for a picnic, which was a foreign concept to Cougar. But he liked the way she hustled around the kitchen, checking in with him to find out whether he liked this or that. He tried to tell her he wasn't picky, but she kept asking, and he kept saying "Sounds good" until she had that canvas lunch bag so full she could hardly close it.

Celia was able to walk right up to the big gray gelding she would be riding, but Cougar had to throw a loop over the buckskin he was assigned. Celia wasn't going to let him saddle her horse for her until he claimed it to be a man's duty according to his tradition. He didn't know whether he was feeding her a line—he figured saddling a woman's horse had to be covered in some soldier, cowboy or Indian code of conduct—but the way she bought into it made him feel good.

The horses were two of Sally's favorites. Tank—the big gray—was the only horse Celia would ride. He'd been Sally's first adoption, and he was a good example of the mustang-draft horse cross that had developed when farmers had opened the gates and turned their plow horses free to fend for themselves. Hostile times, hard times, changing times, the horse had survived it all.

So far.

Cougar rode Little Henry, a horse that liked to play. He was exactly the ride Cougar needed. Coming home to find that he no longer owned a horse had been a staggering blow, the bullet that broke the soldier's heart. *Hoka hey!* he'd cried. *It's a good day to die!* He'd flipped out, gone on a killer drunk, ended up behind bars and then behind locked doors on the psych ward.

And all he'd really needed was a playful horse and a good day to ride.

Celia's ponytail bobbing around up ahead of him was a nice bonus. The way it swished back and forth from shoulder to beautiful bare shoulder was an unexpected turn-on. His little buckskin danced beneath him, eager to pass the big gray, but there was no way

Cougar was giving up this view. It took them nearly an hour to reach their destination.

Time well spent.

"There it is," Celia said of the grassland beyond the three-strand barbwire fence. "That's Mary's father's land. Dan Tutan territory. Here at the Double D he's known as Damn Tootin'. He's one of those ranchers who think any grassland that's not being used by cattle is wasted."

"In Wyoming it's any land without an oil or gas well." Cougar rested his forearm across the saddle horn and drank in the view. He was not a desert man. He'd take rugged mountains, high plains, river bottom breaks or prairie sod over never-ending sand any day. Even in late summer shades of green and brown, an endless expanse of living, breathing, gently swaying grass was a beautiful thing. "You know how people say nothing's sacred anymore?" he mused. "If that's true, guys like that are probably way ahead of the game."

Her voice slid up behind him coupled with the warm breeze. "What game?"

"Whoever dies with the most kills wins."

"Is this a video game or a war game?"

"Doesn't matter. It's always open season, and every hit counts. You choose your—what do they call it? Avatar? Driller and grass grabber must do okay, and it sounds like Mary's father is still rackin' up points." He turned to her, adjusting the brim of his hat against the sun. "Once you're into it, you can find all kinds of ways to play."

"What about you? Are you in the running?"

"I thought I was. Tried to be." He smiled

a little, remembering the gung-ho would-be warrior who'd once greeted him in the mirror. "But I was only going after the bad guys, you know? Only the ones who wore the bad-guy outfits and carried the bad-guy flags."

"What happened?"

"I ran into a little trouble." He sighted down the fence line. "Is that a wire down?"

"Good eye," she said as she tapped the gray with her heel, wheeling him toward the loose wire, no further questions asked. "It's only one wire," she called back to him.

"Can't be the spot we're looking for, but we'll fix it."

Celia dismounted and started untying the tool bag from Cougar's saddle. He reached back and pulled the slipknot on the other side of the saddle skirt.

"You sure tie a tight knot," Celia grumbled. He turned, took the slip string from her hand and gave it a quick jerk. She looked up, squinting against the sun or frowning at him, he wasn't sure which.

He gave her a proper wink. "I sure do."

"I hope that means you can stretch a tight wire."

"I'll stretch it as tight as you want, but—" They both grabbed for the slipping tool bag, and their fingers overlapped. For an instant neither of them moved. "Just don't ask me to walk it," he finished quietly.

"No," she said, quieter still. "I wouldn't."

He gave a little on the bag. "Got it?"

She nodded, and he pulled the saddle strings

out of the way. He dismounted, took a pair of leather gloves from the canvas bag, and they set to work on the barbed wire. Few words were exchanged other than "Hold this," and "Hand me that." He gave no thought to what she might be thinking. Watching her hands move, catching the expression on her face when she watched him, simply being with her filled his head completely. How long had it been since his head had been filled so agreeably?

When the work was done they stood back and admired it, as though they'd created something truly outstanding. They looked at each other and nodded.

"We'll report this to Sally and chalk up some points," Celia said. "Makes it worth the ride even if we don't find a real opening in the fence."

"Riding is worth the ride." Cougar adjusted his hat. "Riding in good company is even better."

"Agreed." She glanced away quickly. "Ready for lunch?"

Figuring they might be getting on each other's nerves in a good way, Cougar reconsidered the sea of grass. A single cottonwood tree beckoned from Tutan territory. "Where's a good hole in the fence when you need one?"

"You'd trespass for one skinny tree?"

"Damn tootin'."

Celia laughed. "What counts as a 'kill'? If it's the same as a coup, you could score two in one day."

"It's part of my nature to be satisfied with

counting coups as kills, but in the army, a coup doesn't earn you any feathers." Cougar gave a tight smile. "Uncle Sam issues you an M16, a near miss gets you nothing but dead."

"You've turned in your combat gear," she reminded him.

"Yeah, but I was trained to trespass." He stepped into the stirrup and swung into his saddle. "I'm still getting used to civilian rules. Transitioning, they call it."

Her saddle creaked as she pulled leather and hauled herself onto the big gray's back. Cougar mentally whipped himself for not offering a leg-up. *Civilian rules.*

"Is everything knotted up nice and tight?" She shaded her eyes with one hand and pointed to the next rolling hill with the other.

"First one gets to the top without losing tools or lunch wins."

He grinned. "Say when."

The big gray beat the little buckskin with an easy, long-legged lope. Cougar called Celia the winner and counted himself a civilian gentleman, at least for one day. The draw below the hill not only offered better shade than the lone tree on the other side of the fence, but an end to their search. They could see a break in the fence at the top of the next hill.

Celia's canvas saddlebags yielded sandwiches, fruit, water and cookies, which she laid out on a faded blue bandanna-print tablecloth on the shady side of a thorny buffalo berry thicket. Cougar loosened the saddles and staked the horses in a shady spot. He plucked a few berries.

"They're not ripe yet," Celia said.

"I know. I used to have to pick these for one of my grammas. It wasn't my favorite chore, but it was worth it for her jelly. She made pemmican, too."

"Must be a lot of work. They're so small." She took off her boots and socks and settled cross-legged, showing off toenails painted the same color as the tablecloth. "They grow in Wyoming?"

"Uh-huh. Ever been to the western part of the state?"

"I haven't traveled much since I moved here from Iowa." Grass crackled beneath the cloth as she patted an empty corner. "Come sit with me."

"More sitting?" He chuckled as he squatted on his heels. He didn't much like eating on the ground anymore, but he liked the way she phrased the invitation. "Why not? Indian style for you, and cowboy style for me."

"What makes that cowboy style?"

"Saddle sores." He raised a cautionary finger as she handed him a sandwich. "Never sit cowboy style with your spurs on."

"Really? Saddle sores?"

He shook his head, laughing. "Not yet. Can't find my spurs, and I haven't ridden a lot lately, so who knows?" He nodded toward her feet. "Were you standing in your stirrups?"

"My toes need a breather. They hate shoes."

"Shoes, yeah, but those are boots. They're not even related." He grinned. "Cute toes."

"You like?" She wiggled all ten. "Mark

painted them for me. Blue is his favorite color."

"Kid's got a future in, uh…"

"Cosmetology?" She offered Cougar a bottle of water. "He wants to fly airplanes. It's been a while since he's talked about it, of course, but he still cruises around the backyard with his arms outstretched." She demonstrated with arms stiff, eyes closed, face lifted toward the sky. The tip of her nose and the high points of her cheeks were pink. "It could happen. Modern medicine, you know, new miracles every day." She opened her eyes suddenly. "How's your sandwich?"

He took a bite, but he couldn't taste anything with the boy gliding silently through his head and the woman tugging on his heartstrings. He nodded and gave her a thumbs-up.

"How did you get involved with the sanctuary?" he asked after some quiet time had passed. He'd finished his sandwich and stretched out in the grass. "Through the Drexlers or the horses?"

"Through my son."

She was ready to tell him. Where he came from, people listened without staring the speaker in the eye, but he could feel her need to exchange signals the way her people did, through the eyes. Hers were frank and fragile. All he knew about his was that, like his ears, they were open.

"The accident happened three years ago. He went through surgery three times and therapy...all kinds of therapy. We were running out of options. Sally's sister, Ann— Did I mention we both teach at the school in Sinte?

Anyway, Ann suggested I bring him out there to see the horses. He took to them immediately."

"Maybe the horses took to him."

Celia smiled. "You sound like Logan. He says things like that in his book. You know, that horses relate to people the way they relate to each other and that they're very sensitive to people who are open to...equine vibes." She shrugged, laughed self-consciously. "Something like that."

"But you're not a believer."

"I want to be. I *desperately* want to be. So far, no one can tell me why Mark doesn't hear or speak or what can be done about it. They tell me it's probably psychosomatic, which usually puts him in some kind of a program, some new and different kind of treatment, some complicated insurance category. I don't care what they say, Mark doesn't hear, and he is unable to speak. I haven't found anyone who relates to him any better than the horses here do." She glanced at the two that grazed nearby. "But they don't speak to me, either, so I can't tell what's going on."

"Give him time."

"I have. I bring him here as often as I can. It's good for both of us. But I have to find a better doctor, a better...something."

"You...wanna tell me what happened?"

"We were with a friend who was having a house built. She was showing me around— this goes here, that goes there—and I was really into it, sort of building my dream house vicariously. Mark was almost six. Curious about everything, you know? He was, um...

he put his eye over a hole…in a floor…and someone who was working down below…" She held an imaginary dagger in her fisted hand and thrust upward.

Cougar braced for the blow he'd lived and relived, the white heat of stabbing steel, the breathtaking terror, the staggering pain. As long as he was awake and in control of his faculties he could hold himself together and let it pass through him. The physical pain in his own body always turned out to be bearable, but it was everything that went with it—all the jacks in the boxes, ghosts in the closet—the doubts were what kept him up at night.

"It was a metal rod." She spoke softly, for which he was grateful. "It took the eye, every bit of it, but nothing more. It could have been so much worse."

Questions sprang to mind, but he ignored them. She would have been asked more times than she could count, and she would have answered and answered and answered. But she would never be sure of anything except that she could have done something differently. And every time she replayed the incident, she would try something else, and it would always change the outcome for the better.

He reached for the hand she held fisted on her knee, uncurled her fingers with a gently probing thumb as he drew it to him and pressed his lips to her palm.

"I know," she said, barely audibly. "It's over. Just breathe."

"It sounds easy." He closed his hand around hers and smiled sadly. *"I know."*

Chapter Four

Celia sat on the front step watching each little vehicle as it appeared on the hill half a mile away and slid down the highway. Watching traffic was relaxing when Mark was home. Passing cars were few and far between on their remote highway—a welcome change from their apartment overlooking a busy street in Des Moines—and Celia had made up several guessing games for them to play on summer evenings. Mark loved anything with paws, hooves, wheels or wings, and Celia loved anything that made Mark happy.

Mark's father was not one of those things, and watching for his delivery truck was not relaxing.

A house full of silence had her back. She would take Mark from Greg's clutches, thank him very much, go inside and close the door. Still quiet but not utterly silent, the house would surround them and keep him out for two blessed weeks. She loved her new house. It was only new to Celia—certainly nothing fancy—but the walls were solid and the doors had locks. And it was *hers*. The mortgage was in her name. She'd bought the house and forty-two acres of grass land in an estate auction, and she'd spent the past six months struggling to fix the place up.

Celia took off her gardening gloves, laid them beside the clay pot she'd just filled with mums and rubbed her hands together. One palm felt warmer than the other. She turned it up, imagined a lip imprint and smiled to herself. It was one of many places she'd never been kissed, and she'd been deeply touched by the gesture. Prickles-in-the-throat touched. Butterflies-deep-in-the-belly touched. Cougar was anything but a cool cat. He was warm and sensitive, a little mysterious, *a lot* attractive, a surprise at every turn.

She would see him tonight at the powwow grounds. Just thinking about it made her feel like a teenager.

But waiting for Greg made her feel anxious and worn out at the same time. Their marriage had been over before Mark's accident. He'd never taken much interest in Mark even though he liked to say he was looking forward to riding bikes with his son or playing ball or having some real conversation. As soon as Mark got over being a baby, they were going to be great buddies. Mark's milestones passed without Greg's notice, while Celia's every move was closely monitored. Who was that on the phone? Why was she showing off her boobs in that dress? What was she really doing when she said she was taking the baby to the park? Celia signed them up for counseling, but the handwriting was on the wall.

The accident made it official. Celia had done the unthinkable. She'd dropped the ball. God only knew what she was doing when she was supposed to be watching, but Mark was broken beyond repair. Now it was one surgery after another, more doctors, more treatment plans, more sleepless nights. Greg had no stomach for "medical stuff," and he had all but taken his leave. He cut his visitations or skipped out on them altogether. But that was before the "know your rights" guy had stepped in.

The sight of the bread truck sent dour memories packing. As soon as the truck stopped, Mark was out the door and in her arms.

Greg strolled up behind him. "We didn't get to the Reptile Gardens, but we did some other stuff. We hit Mickey D's a couple of times." He ruffled Mark's hair. "Didn't we, son? Golden arches?" He whistled as his hand dove over an air arch. "They had a play-ground. Good times, huh?"

"I missed you, Markie-B. You had fun?" Celia touched his chin, and he turned to her with a smile. "You and your dad had fun?"

"Are you hoping he'll say *no?*"

"I'm hoping he'll say something. I don't care what it is." She kissed the top of his head. "You will. I know you will."

"What have you heard from the insurance company?"

And there it was. Greg's new baby's name was Lawsuit.

Greg's renewed interest in Mark had been clear from the moment he'd followed Celia to South Dakota and petitioned for the visitation rights he'd shrugged off when they'd divorced. With the help of his new ambulance-chasing lawyer—he relished saying the words *my lawyer*—Greg had claimed Celia wasn't looking after Mark's best interests in court, any more than—according to Greg— she had looked after his safety the day he'd been injured. The medical bills had been covered, and Celia agreed that there was no way of knowing what other needs might arise for Mark in the future. But there was a sure way of knowing what Greg was up to. All it took was watching him operate.

Celia could think of nothing she'd rather do less.

"I'm sure the insurance company has your lawyer on speed dial," she said. "Or *vice versa*."

"I have a feeling you'll hear first. You still have everyone thinking you're Saint Cecilia."

"As far as I know they're still dickering."

"Cheap bastards," he spat. "We should get… You know, *Mark* should get millions. You hear about multi-million dollar damage awards every day."

"I don't want to talk about this, Greg. Not now."

"Don't you want our son to get what's coming to him?"

"That's what the lawyers are for." She put her arm around Mark's shoulders and turned to mount the steps. "We'll see you in—"

"What's with the Indian guy?" he said quietly. "How long has that been going on?"

She stopped between steps.

"Not that it's any of my business, you and him, but he nearly ran over my kid. That's my business."

Fortunately, Celia, you're the only one who can hear him. Go inside.

"If he's in such a killing hurry to get to you that he'll mow down anything that gets in his way—" his shoe—one shoe—scraped the gravel "—and it's my kid that's in his way, you damn well bet that's my business."

"Don't threaten me, Greg." She opened the front door and nudged Mark inside before turning to face him. "I *will* get a restraining order."

"How did I threaten you? What did I say? I'm not touching you. All I'm saying is that I will protect my son."

Celia stepped inside.

"Somebody has to." Greg wedged the words in edgewise through the shrinking crack as she closed the door.

Mark put his arms around her and hugged her.

"We're fine, Markie-B." She rubbed his back. "You and me, babe. We're going to…" She lifted his chin. "Look at me. We're going to a party tonight. We're going to have supper, and there'll be lots of kids. I think there will. *Of course,* there will. It's a celebration. *And…*" She smiled. "You remember Cougar? He'll be there. We like him, don't we?"

She went on chattering the way she had done when he was a baby, without talking down to or babbling at him. He was a person, and he was present, and he would soon participate in the conversation. It was more than a wish on her part. It was an expectation. She talked about horseback riding and fixing fences and Bridget the cat going hunting again and catching a mouse in the tack room.

Mark was eager to throw his clothes in the laundry room, shower and wash his hair. While he was in the bathroom she checked his clothes. They reeked of cigarette smoke. Greg wasn't a smoker. She had the feeling the weekend entertainment—likely involving gambling—had not been kid-friendly.

She wasn't going to grill Mark about it. He was glad to be home, and he didn't need to be asked questions he couldn't or wouldn't answer. But she wished they could go back to the days when an occasional supervised visit with his son was all Greg had time for.

Mark emerged from the bathroom looking handsome in his khaki shorts and polo shirt, light brown hair all slicked down. Little gentleman that he was, he opened the front door for his mom. But rather than follow her, he ran back into his room.

He'd changed his mind. He'd had enough socializing. He didn't understand what was going on. He *did* understand, and he wanted no part of it. Celia was trying to learn new signs and signals, but she would have given anything for a word from her son. One word, one...

...foot in front of the other, scurrying down the hallway, bringing her a boy who'd almost forgotten his favorite red baseball cap, which he never took with him when he went with his father. He was giving her all the signs and signals a mother could want in one beautiful gap-toothed smile.

* * *

It was a quiet, stonewash denim sky evening. The sun had lost its command, and the swallows were gaining on the mosquitoes. Somebody was testing out a microphone, somebody else toying with a drumbeater as Celia parked her car in the grassy parking area at the powwow grounds. She didn't see Cougar's pickup, and she gave herself a mental scolding. She knew she would have parked near him, as close as she could get, and she felt silly about it. Eager and silly. *Totally regressive, Celia.*

Kinda fun, though.

But his mean-looking black pickup wasn't there. Maybe he wasn't coming.

"Hey, you made it."

Celia whirled toward the sound of the voice

and found Cougar striding toward her. He looked wonderful in a crisp white Western shirt, sleeves rolled just above his wrists, and a pair of Wranglers he was clearly wearing for the first time.

Mark accepted Cougar's handshake without hesitation, man to man. He greeted Celia with a hand press. She didn't want him to let go. His eyes said he got it, and his smile said he was glad of it.

"Lots of people here," Cougar said as he touched the small of her back. She took Mark's hand, and they started walking toward the bowery, the big circular structure—open in the center, thatched with leafy cottonwood branches around the perimeter—that had stood for ceremony and celebration for the

Lakota since before recorded memory. "You probably know most of them."

"I know more kids than adults. I teach sixth graders. I know some parents. I've met Mary once at the Double D." Celia nodded toward the far side of the arena, where familiar faces were sharing animated conversation. "There she is, over there with the Drexler crew. Except Sally and Ann are no longer Drexlers. I wonder where Ann is." She was rattling on awkwardly. She never missed a school function, but her social calendar was pretty empty. "Have you met Ann Beaudry, Sally's sister? We both..."

"Teach," Cougar remembered, smiling. "You've mentioned that a few times. You must really enjoy it."

"Most days I do. I struggled the first year,

but now that I have a few years' experience under my belt, I think I'm getting pretty good at it."

"Is that what that bulge is?" He dropped the smile and gave a chin jerk toward her small waist. "I was wondering."

Celia laid her hand over her belt buckle and gave him the squint-eye.

"Mrs. Banyon!" Celia turned to greet a bright-eyed girl with a sagging ponytail. "We're playing dodge ball. Can your son play?"

"Dodge ball?" She glanced at Mark, who was playing on the bench with a Matchbox airplane. "I don't know, hon, that's so dangerous."

"We'll be careful," the girl promised. "We're using a soft ball."

"A softball?"

"A *soft* ball. It's practically a cotton ball, it's so soft." She looked up at Cougar. "It's the only one we could find."

"It's so nice of you to include Mark, but you know, his eye…"

"I'll make sure he doesn't get hurt." She leaned sideways to peek at Mark's face. "I'm gonna be in your class next year, Mrs. Banyon."

Logan joined them, laughing as he laid a hand on the girl's shoulder. "So there's no way Maxine's gonna let anything happen to your son. I'll vouch for her. She's my niece's kid. The Indian way, that makes her my granddaughter. Right, Maxine?" He winked at Celia. "Last week she told me to stop calling her Maxie."

"Geez, Lala Logan. That's so embarrassing."

"I didn't know. I'm just a man." Logan gently tugged Maxine's ponytail. He nodded toward the long serving table the younger women and teens were loading up with kettles and pans. "Why don't you take Mark over to get some chow? The kids are lining up. Go ask Grandma Margaret whether she wants you to help with the little ones or take plates to the elders."

Maxine folded her arms and glared at the row of chairs holding elders-in-waiting near the serving table. "I'm helping the kids."

"What happened?"

She gave a nod toward the group. "That one said I walk like a duck."

Celia couldn't tell from the gesture whether

the wizened woman with the black scarf tied over her head or the leathery man with the walker was the deadpan tease.

"Do you?" Logan asked.

"No!"

"Then don't worry about it. He used to tell me I walked like a bear."

"Are Ann and Zach here?" Celia asked on the tail end of the laughter.

"I saw them somewhere." Logan glanced over his shoulder and forgot who he was looking for. "Hey, here's my decorated warrior."

Dressed in Army green, Sergeant Mary Wolf Track took her husband's hand and stood by his side. "And I see Cougar's already made a friend," Mary said, offering her free hand. "Celia, right? You volunteer at the Double D."

"She's a teacher," Cougar put in. "When I

signed up for the wild horse training competition, that quick, Sally had her teaching me
how to fix fence."

"Cougar's the one who deserves the medal,"
Mary told Celia, as though he needed a reference. "He might not be a soldier anymore,
but this man is one brave cowboy."

"More like a cowboy brave," Cougar said
diffidently.

"A cowboy brave. Now there's a... What's
that called?" Mary snapped her fingers and
pointed at Celia. "Teacher?"

"An oxymoron." Celia smiled. "Just remember *stupid laundry soap.*"

"Ignore them." Logan clapped a hand on
Cougar's shoulder. "Either way, you're the
man. When we turn on the mike, would you
step up first?"

"You said you'd keep it simple," Mary pleaded.

"That's just me," Logan told his wife. "Can't speak for everybody here." He turned to Cougar. "She just married into an Indian family. She's got a lot to learn."

"He's a tribal councilman," Cougar told Mary. "Sure sign he never met a microphone he didn't like."

Logan laughed. "The Shoshone are well known for their pretty faces and their coarse tongues."

"The Lakota are just the opposite," Cougar said. "Scary faces and silver tongues."

"The way I heard it, you're part Lakota," Logan said.

Cougar smiled. "I got the best of both worlds."

"Get yourselves something to eat," Logan

said. "I can't wait to hear this guy put his money where his mouth is."

Celia was thinking the same thing. Cougar didn't strike her as the speech-making type, but he spoke of his fellow soldier—he called her an outstanding warrior—from the heart. She was a dog handler and trainer, and when the time came, Cougar spoke reverently of the lives Mary's dogs had saved. The handlers in his MP unit "talked up their Tutan-trained dogs like they were smarter than the average GI. And the average GI wholeheart-edly agrees."

There were several testimonials, including one from Mary's shy but very proud mother, but there were even more expressions of appreciation and camaraderie in arms from veterans. Celia had heard about the generations of American Indians who had served in the military, but she was seeing the evidence, hearing the voices for the first time. She paid close attention and mentally recorded each comment having to do with a way of life that hadn't really touched her until now. For all her close listening and mental note-taking, her thoughts were with Cougar. What was he remembering? How did he feel about it?

She felt chosen when he came to get Mark and her for the Honor Song. They cued up behind the VFW color guard, followed by Mary and her husband and family. The slow iambic cadence of the drum echoed the earth's heartbeat, and the procession grew. The singers pitched their voices ever higher, calling the stars, one by one, to the purpling sky.

And then came the dancing. The young

Fancy Dancers' colorful feather bustles covered their back from head to toe, and when they twirled it was like watching a spinning carnival ride. Shawl Dancers used their flashy fringed shawls to create wings worthy of hovering on the wind, and the Traditional Dancers' porcupine roach headdresses bobbed in perfect imitation of a tall grass prairie chicken all puffed up and "booming" to attract female attention.

"Look at Mark." Cougar laid his hand on Celia's knee and nodded toward the drum circle, where children gathered like groupies.

Mark was dancing! He was imitating the other boys—whirling, stomping, nodding like a playful grouse—but he was moving in perfect rhythm with the drum.

"Pretty damn good," Cougar said. "How long has he been at it?"

Celia couldn't take her eyes off her son. She shook her head slightly, spoke softly, as though he might hear her and feel self-conscious. Her heart fluttered wildly. "He's never done it before."

"He's sure feelin' it."

"That's it, isn't it? He feels the drum." Not quite the same as hearing it, but it was an acknowledgment, wasn't it? He was being reached. "I dance with him at home, but he just stumbles around. It must be the live music. The bass drum. I should've tried this before."

"Haven't you been to a powwow?"

"We've been to a couple, but only to watch.

We sat on the bleachers. This is the first time he's..."

"First time you've let him get in there with the kids?"

She glanced at him warily. "I try to keep a close watch on him. I really do."

"Anybody can see that, Celia. Anybody with honest eyes." He smiled and nodded toward the clutch of kids. "Either Maxine's trying to make some points with you, or she's a little mother hen. Probably both, huh?"

"A little prairie chicken hen, right?" Her shoulders settled down. She hadn't even realized she'd hiked them up. He had a way of smoothing her ruffled feathers with a single stroke.

She laid her hand over his. "Do you have children?"

"Nope."

"You connect with them. Most men don't unless they have their own."

"Really?"

"Some don't, even if they have their own." She tipped her head back and gave a small, sardonic laugh. "I'm sorry. I'm making generalizations. I don't know what I'm talking about."

He turned his palm to hers and closed his hand around hers slowly. "You see the people hangin' outside the bowery?"

She glanced over her shoulder, between a couple of droopy branches and into the dusky perimeter. Shadows strolling, shadows giggling and chasing shadows. Shadows loitering and lingering in tête-à-tête pose.

Celia smiled. "Ah, yes."

"There's some old-fashioned courting going on out there."

"I thought this represented courting." She nodded toward the dancers.

"It does if you're a bird." He laughed. "I tried Fancy Dancing, but with two left feet, I was the one who laid an egg. Picked myself up off the ground, climbed on a horse and suddenly the chicks noticed me."

"And you were how old?"

"About fifteen." He squeezed her hand. "What else do you wanna know? I don't have a wife, or an ex-wife or a girlfriend. I do have an ex-girlfriend." He lifted one shoulder. "She got tired of waiting. Can't blame her."

Holding hands. She was holding hands with a man, and her insides were jitterbugging. *Ask an intelligent question, Celia.*

"How long were you over in the Middle East?"

"Altogether, thirty-two months."

"That would be hard on a relationship."

"Some people have done three, even four tours between Iraq and Afghanistan. People who have families at home..." He glanced across the circle. Arm in arm, Mary and Logan were receiving well wishers. "...should be with their families. I could do another tour, easy. So somebody with a family could come home."

"Do you want to go back?"

"I don't know where I want to be. Except maybe..." He turned to her, looked into her through her eyes in a way that thrilled and terrified her. She was the connection he had on his mind, and she wasn't sure he wanted it there. But there it was.

He cocked his head toward the perimeter. "Care to go for a stroll?"

She wanted to look away from the eyes that held hers, check with Mark, find something to hold her back, but she couldn't. The look in his eyes shifted from challenging to amused.

"He's still there."

She smiled. "Still dancing?"

"Still dancing. Havin' a hell of a time."

She stood up from the end of the bench, and he followed suit. She gave his hand a squeeze. "You're making a statement here."

"*You're* making a statement, teacher." He gave a return squeeze as they emerged from the bowery onto the beaten path. "Nobody knows me here. I am—what's the expression? *Off the reservation.*"

"But this *is* the reservation," she accommodated him, laughing.

"Not mine. But, hey." He leaned down close to her ear. "Let 'em talk. I ain't afraid of Indian country."

"Off the reservation," she echoed as they strolled. "Indian country. Does any of that bother you?"

"You know what bothers me? Chief. I don't wanna be called *chief.* First sergeant was good enough. Any rank with *chief* attached..." He shook his head.

"How about commander-in-chief?"

"They couldn't call me *chief,* then, could they?"

"Have they always just called you Cougar?"

"Nope." He looked at her, and for a moment she thought he might tell her his secret. Or one of them. He grinned. "But they do now."

She glanced into the bowery as they passed the drum circle. There was Mark trying out a new step, and there was Maxine, tending to her assignment.

"Hey." Cougar tugged on her hand. "It's our turn to swing."

"What?" She stumbled over the angle her sudden pivot required. "We're walkin' here," she quipped.

"Did you see this?" He led her down a small grassy slope, jumped a dry washout and scrambled up the other side,

She couldn't see anything. The stars were out, the horizon held on to a rosy sliver of leftover sunset, and the moon had yet to show its face.

"Do you have night vision?"

"Of course."

Now she saw a huge, dark, hulking tree. It wasn't until he grabbed something hanging from it, tugged and didn't detect any give that she realized what kind of swinging he had in mind. He assessed the distance from the ground to the thick, wide plank seat, muttered, "Too low," and tossed the seat over the branch that held it until the length of the ropes met his requirements.

"I can't wait to see you climb up there and fix it when you're finished playing," she said.

"Don't hold your breath." He gave the ropes a firm tug.

"But what about the kids?"

"They'll fight over who gets to make the climb."

"Somebody might fall."

"I never did." He took a seat. "How much do you weigh?"

"Two-twenty. What's it to ya?" She grabbed the rope, stacking her hand on top of hi, and circled toward his back. "I'll start you off with one push, but then—"

He caught her at the waist with a long shepherd's crook of an arm. "Come sit on my lap and let's ride double." He drew her to stand between his knees. "This is a two-passenger swing. They don't make 'em like this anymore."

"Because seats made out of leftover lumber..." She took a rope in each hand, kicked off her shoes, stepped up and planted a foot on either side of his hips. "…somebody could get hurt." She lowered herself onto his lap.

"Keep most of that two-twenty off somebody, he'll be fine."

She stared at him for a moment. She shouldn't reward such talk. But, then, she shouldn't be sitting on him like this. Her next bold move—tipping his hat back—exposed bright expectation in his eyes. He was waiting. She dropped her head back and laughed.

He took his hat off and tossed it in the grass, pushed off the ground with his booted feet just as she stretched her legs out behind his back. "You're a hundred or so off in your estimate, I'd say."

They were flying low, chasing evening shadows with bright smiles.

She leaned back on the upswing. "This is crazy!"

"You never did this?"

"Okay for two little people, maybe, but this limb could break."

"Pretend we're one big person, and we'll blend." Forward on the backswing, she lent him an ear. "A good tree feels sorry for a kid this heavy—" he nipped her earlobe between whisperings "—coming out here all alone in the dark—" nuzzled her cheek "—looking to take a few minutes' flight."

His first kiss came mid-flight. Lips to lips only. No hands, no arms. It felt like a warm greeting, a discovery so welcome as to warrant a replay. And another, and another, each tasting sweeter than the last with her sitting on him like this and him growing on her like that. Barely perceptible, a tickle between her legs that begged to be pressed. But the shared awareness and the delicious resistance was worth preserving. A good lover would know that. And Cougar, she now knew, would be such a lover. The lover she'd known in dreams.

They let the motion wind down by slow degrees. Just before standstill he took her face in his hands and kissed her lusciously, thoroughly, to the point of knowing nothing but the joy of kissing.

He touched his forehead to hers, rolled it back and forth, surely leaving an imprint. She hoped it contained that kiss.

"I'll say it for you," he whispered. "This was fun, but you have to get back."

"It was." Her lips brushed his. "I do."

He smiled against her lips. "The next move is all yours."

She laughed. "And there's no graceful way."

But she was barefoot and agile, and she untangled herself from man and swing without losing dignity. Which, surprisingly, she suddenly felt in abundance. Dignity and class and beauty and all kinds of confidence magnified by a simple kiss.

He recovered his hat, and she her shoes, and they walked hand in hand, the bright bowery up ahead. He pointed toward the rear view of a man carrying a child on his back.

"That's Mark!" Celia exclaimed.

"Riding the master trainer," Cougar said with a chuckle as they approached the narrow washout. "Kid's got style."

"How long have we been gone? Ouch!" She grabbed for his arm. "I lost my shoe."

"I see it." He bent to retrieve her comfy, clunky slip-on. "You do know this is boot country."

"They're hard to take off."

"Let's see if I can lift two-twenty."

He gave her the shoe, and she laughed as he swept her up in his arms, jumped the narrow crevasse and scaled the grassy slope in three steps.

"Wow, you really *are* strong." And they were getting closer to the bowery. "Now, if your manly ears have heard enough music, please put me down before someone sees us."

He stopped short. "Too much style?"

"A little overstated." She kissed him sweetly. "But thank you."

He lowered her to the ground and into her shoe, and they lingered a moment longer, a pair of outsiders clinging to each other in the dark like children reluctant to go in for the night. They watched Maxine lay claim to Mark while Logan grabbed his wife's hand for the *kahamni,* the traditional Lakota circle dance.

"I know where I don't wanna be tonight," Cougar said, picking up on the question she'd asked earlier. He jerked his chin toward the Wolf Tracks as they sidestepped out of view. "And that's camping out in their backyard. She's home on a three-day pass."

"I have a huge yard," she offered, sounding more eager than she'd intended. "Is that all you need? I have electricity and running water, too. And an old barn." Eagerness shamelessly amplified, she thought. "And most of a corral. It's only missing a few pieces."

He grinned. "Are you offering me a place to park?"

"A place to camp." She lifted one shoulder. "At least as long as Mary's home. I'm sure you'll want to go back to their place to work on your program."

"For sure. Gotta work my program."

"But it looks as though the honeymoon is still on." The couple had danced back into view on the far side of the circle. "It's really no trouble."

"I'll pay you," he said.

"I'll take that offer as acceptance of mine. No strings attached." She glanced over her shoulder toward the silhouette of their tree.

"I don't know about where you come from, but we don't charge for parking in these parts. One thing we have in South Dakota is plenty of parking space."

"Just because I let you kiss me doesn't mean I'm looking for favors."

She turned back with a mock scowl. "*Let me—*"

"I don't mind paying in services. So what can I do you for?"

"How good are you with tools?"

"I'm a man. I know tools. What do you need?"

"What *don't* I need? I bought a fixer-upper and a few acres of pasture in an estate sale. The farm land was sold separately, and nobody wanted the home place. Nobody but me.

But there's more to this fixing up business than I thought."

"Now we're on the same side. No confusion. We both know what's on the table." He offered his hand. "You got yourself a deal."

Chapter Five

Dust billowing around the truck made it hard to see where he was going, but he couldn't slow down now. If he did, something bad would happen. There were people out there, faces looming in the dust clouds, but they didn't matter as long as they stayed clear of the truck. He had to get to a place where he wasn't eating dirt every time he tried to take a breath or say a word.

Sand.

The place was made of sand. Grittier than Wyoming dust, sharper sting in the eye, bigger clog in the nose, worse threat to the throat. He was fine with faces. He could fire back at bullets. Sand was the enemy. Hot wind and godawful sand.

Suddenly one fiend sucked the other up, and the faces were unveiled. Unreadable eyes, most of them, all but the children. He slowed down for the children. They were dancing, whirling like the wind, arms outstretched like little airplanes, eyes bright.

Eyes right. Right side of the road, right here right now, pedestrians have the right of way. Right foot, Cougar, brake right.

Don't stop for anything, Sergeant. That

kid's coming for us. You slow down, he takes us out. Do. Not. Stop.

Cougar sat up screaming. Shaking, shooting out of the sandbox like a bottle rocket and screaming to beat hell. He knocked the blind off the window and hit his head on the ceiling above the trailer's loft bed. He was in for a killing headache.

Headaches don't kill people. People kill people.

Head noise killed sleep. Cougar couldn't remember his last full night of quiet sleep. The first part of the night almost wasn't worth the last part, but a guy had to take what he could get. Otherwise the hole got deeper and the walls felt tighter.

He went to his medicine chest and sorted through his options. He kept them all handy these days. Pills, packaged injections, a pint of whiskey, a pack of cigarettes. He'd used them all. He wanted to be free of them all. "It's a process," the doctors kept telling him. And banging his head against the wall—ceiling, whatever—was part of it.

He grabbed two bottles—pills and booze—pulled his boots on, burst out the side door and into the vast and velvety night. He set the bottles side by side on top of a fencepost and backed away. Maybe the fresh air would do it. Maybe all he needed was wide open spaces and a chill chaser. He went back for the pint, uncapped it, drew a long, deep breath full of whiskey fumes and capped it back up again.

"Are you okay?"

Cougar spun on his heel, crouching like a Hollywood gunfighter.

Celia squared up, looking surprised, like he'd been the one who'd just sneaked up on her. He straightened slowly. His reaction was nothing to be embarrassed about. Hell, he was glad to know that getting himself locked away by the white coats hadn't dulled his reflexes too much. As long as he wasn't looking for anything sharp or loaded, he was doing fine.

"I'm sorry," she said quickly. She was clutching a small, fringed blanket around her shoulders, and her legs were bare.

He gave a dry chuckle. "What for? Catching me in the act?"

"Of..."

He gestured with the bottle. "I have orders to stay away from this stuff."

"Orders from whom?" She tipped her head

to one side, as though she'd just asked whether he'd rather have a glass of warm milk.

"*Whom?* I like that. Whom. It sounds proper." He studied the bottle. "Dr. Choi, that's *whom*."

"Which isn't proper, but we won't get into that. You sounded..." She swished through the dry grass toward the fencepost, but she paid no attention to the pills. Instead she peered into the deepest part of the cricket-filled night. "I ran into a badger out here one night. Scared me half to death."

"Did he come after you?"

"He ran one way, and I ran the other." She turned to him, one hand spread over her chest holding the blanket in place. Moonlight washed over her worried face. "Do you mind if I ask why Dr. Choi gave you those orders?"

He nodded toward the pill bottle, poised on the post like a shooting target. "He wants me to take those. He says they'll mix it up with the spirits."

"You mean you're not supposed to mix the medication with spirits?"

"Is that the proper word for booze? Spirits?" He laughed and shook his head. "I don't mind if you ask. You should ask. I'm sleeping in your backyard, and you've got a kid to protect. Not to mention..." He scanned her makeshift cloak, neck to knees, and his imagination shifted into high gear. "Sorry I woke you up."

"You didn't. I was sitting outside." She shrugged. "I heard you, um..."

"Friggin' embarrassing as hell." *Sitting out-*

side? Right. He glanced at the sky. It must have been three in the morning. "I scared you."

"A little. Only because…" She was staring at the bottle in his hand. "It sounded like you were in terrible pain."

"Just a dream." He set the pint back on the fence and stood back. "I don't like taking the pills. They feed the spirits they're supposed to fight off."

"The things that go bump in the night?"

He chuckled as he plowed his fingers though his thick hair. "Yeah, my damn head. I can't get used to that low ceiling."

"Mark has nightmares, too. He crawls in bed with me sometimes, and the only way I know he's crying is that his face is wet."

Cougar froze. Instantly the scene played out in his mind. Screaming, crying, cussing, head-banging—a kid doubled over in terror and none of these outlets were available to him.

He shoved his hands into his pockets. No shirt, but he'd had the presence of mind to keep his jeans on. "You think he hears anything in his dreams?"

"That's a good question." She let the blanket slip as she linked her arm with his. T-shirt and shorts. No bra. His arm was tucked against the side of her breast. "Come sit with me. I can't sleep now, either."

"I could sure sleep if I picked a poison." But he let her lead the way, which was not in poison's direction.

"What woke you up, Cougar? Was there some kind of noise? In your dream, I mean."

"Not exactly. It's hard to tell. Hell, it was a dream."

"If I knew what was going on in Mark's head, maybe I could..." With her free hand she flipped the blanket over her shoulder. "Logan's book is all about understanding what goes on in a horse's head. They can't tell you in words, so you have to pay attention to other signs, other language." Her tone dropped from instructional to personal. "I know what happened, but I didn't actually see it happen."

"Neither did the guy who did it."

"No, he didn't. The poor man, he was devastated. He came to the hospital and just sat there, waiting. He ended up losing his job. There was no warning, no signs, no barriers, but that was the contractor's fault. No one actually saw what happened. Everyone heard him scream."

"You hear it in your dreams?"

She nodded.

"Hey. I'm sorry. Last thing I wanna do is go diggin' around in somebody else's dreams. I know the sound of..." They'd reached the house. He planted a boot on the first rickety step of two leading to the ground-level deck. It squeaked and sagged but didn't crack. He surveyed the deck and noticed crude patches in the planking. "...worn-out wood. Ready to retire."

"I've made some temporary repairs." She pointed to a glider at the far edge of the deck. "That part's pretty sturdy. I covered some holes, and then started replacing planks."

"It won't take much to fix up one of those

pens so I can get started with the mustang. You want me to start on the deck after that? Or do you have something more important that needs doing?" He glanced left and right. "I don't see a swing."

"A swing would be..." She laughed. "Swings can be dangerous. Come try this glider out." She sat down beside him, mentioned the night chill as she tossed the blanket across their laps and pulled her side up to her shoulders. "I don't have many tools, but there's lots of good lumber in the barn. It came with the property. I think I need some sort of an electric saw."

"You did this much with just a handsaw?"

"I found pieces that fit. I looked at saws once, but I couldn't find one that wouldn't cut fingers."

"Did you try the toy department?" With no thought of making a move he reached under the blanket and drew her legs onto his lap. Her feet stuck out, rubber flip-flops dangling off her polish-tipped toes, and her skin felt smooth and cool. "You might as well be walking barefoot on a bed of nails."

"What do you mean? These shoes have great soles."

He groaned. "That's cute, but this is hay needle and prickly pear country. You don't know what you'll run into in the dark."

"When I came outside I wasn't planning to leave the deck." She leaned back for a double take. "You do realize that, don't you?"

"Yeah, but you did. It would've been smarter not to."

"I suppose. But I don't feel stupid." She laughed. "Okay, maybe about the footwear."

He ran his hand over the top of her leg until he reached cloth. "What's this?"

"Pajama shorts," she said in a clipped tone, as though any idiot would know. And then she groaned. "Yes, they're pajamas, but they're also shorts. I'm not running around naked, and I'm not trying to..."

"Seduce me?" He laughed. "It wouldn't take much." His hand retreated to her knee. "I'm just saying you could get hurt. You heard somebody in trouble, and you came running. You don't know what kind of trouble you'll find."

"I know you wouldn't hurt me," she said quietly.

"I wouldn't want to." He lifted his arm over

her head and pushed against the deck with his booted foot. The glider creaked as he set it in motion. "I'd rather rock you gently."

"A swinger and a rocker." She laid her head on his bare shoulder. "Aren't you cold?"

"I woke up in a sweat. The night air is just what the doctor ordered."

"Dr. Choi?"

The question was loaded, and his instinct was to duck. But he let it rest with him for a moment, testing it out. It was heavy, but coming from Celia, it didn't feel like a threat. She'd stuck her neck out saying she believed she was safe with him, and she deserved answers since he was parked in her backyard.

"I got hit in an explosion," he said quietly. "I was lucky. I didn't lose any limbs. Had a little head damage, but it could've been a lot worse." He tipped his head back and drank in more night air. "I won't lie to you, Celia, I was a mess when I came home. When I came *back*. I don't know about home."

"Things had changed?"

"No. Not much. I mean, I thought so at first, but then I realized that life had gone on exactly the way people had been living it before I left. What was I expecting?"

"You felt like a stranger?"

"I was. But it was me. My problem. I felt betrayed, but the truth is, I didn't wanna be with people who'd known me before. I didn't know who I'd become, but I knew I couldn't be that person again. So they were right to move on." He glanced at her and smiled. "And that's a whole lot more than I ever told Dr. Choi."

"It's the glider. It's like a watch on a chain." She mimicked the motion with her hand. "Watch the watch."

"That's the one thing they didn't try on me." He tipped his head back again and kept rocking. "What a night," he said. The moon had disappeared, and there was nothing overhead but an infinite black canvas stippled with stars. There was no yard light, no city, no town, nothing throwing man-made competition up against natural gems. "You know, there are a lot of people who have never seen the Milky Way? Never."

"They see it in Afghanistan, don't they?"

"Oh, yeah. It's almost as pretty as this. Unless you're wearing night vision goggles that turn everything glow-in-the-dark green. Which is fun if you're into video games. You line up a target, you score a hit, you rack up the points. Points, people, whatever. The bad guys." He glanced at her. "The people over there are tribal."

She smiled. "So are yours."

"Shh. Don't tell anybody." He looked up again, still rocking, his hand stirring over her smooth skin. Two strangers in a strange land, he thought. Somehow they were able to cut through the chaos and see each other clearly. "What a night," he said again.

"Shooting star!" She pointed to a ribbon of fire streaking across the sky. "Did you make a wish?"

He shook his head. "It's a gift. Halfway around the world you see something like that, it clears your head." He smiled against the night. "*Look at me,* it says. *I'm going down in a blaze of glory.* And everybody gets the same gift. You don't have to fight over it."

"Even so, a girl can wish."

"If it has anything to do with this deck, I can tear it out and replace it in a day or two, depending on what's under there for footings." He ran his hand along her shin and closed it around her slender ankle and gave a playful shake. "If it's as flimsy as these shoes…"

"Stop knocking my shoes." Laughing, she started to pull away, but he held on until she looked up. "You don't scare me, Cougar."

"That makes one of us," he said as he lowered his head and went in for a kiss.

He knew he was hungry for the taste of her, but he thought he could sate himself with just that—a taste. Even if he couldn't, he would make do, maybe take a little more, a touch of the tongue, a nip of the lip. He drew breath from her breath as he slid his hand up slowly, stretching his fingers to accommodate the widening of her thigh, feeling every fine hair, sensing her excitement. He paused when he encountered clothing, deepened his kiss and let his fingers slide farther until he felt the catch in her breath, and then he stayed his hand as he kissed her through the moment.

"Two of us now," she whispered when she could.

"I'll stop."

"That's what I'm afraid of."

He kissed her again while his fingers explored the swell of her hip, the peak of her pelvis, and the dip into her belly. His thumb found coarse hair marking another peak, a hard place, a protective boundary. The feel of her all-over, deep-down trembling thrilled him, pushing for quick, decisive action. It pleased him to test his own resistance even as he challenged hers.

He rubbed her belly. "I don't make wishes," he whispered, and he tried to offer up a smile with his little joke, but it wouldn't come.

"I do." She touched his cheek. "But...I can't..."

"I know."

He knew what?

Celia lay on her bed staring at the ceiling, enjoying the instant replay. All but the talk. And wasn't that a fine how-do-you-do? Yes, indeed, she made wishes, and one of them involved heartfelt words. He'd talked. He'd told her things he hadn't told anyone else. All she'd said was that he didn't scare her, and he knew that.

What else did he know?

That she couldn't believe how potent his kiss was? That she couldn't believe the urgency it made her feel, the need to reach out and hold on and kiss back? That she couldn't believe the power of a little pleasure, couldn't ask him to make love to her, couldn't stop thinking he should stop and hoping he wouldn't?

Of course he knew all that.

But did he know she wasn't really a flirt? If he thought about it, it was probably pretty obvious, considering how inept she was at it. Could he tell how happy she was to have him there and how upset she was with herself for showing it? She'd been feeling alone

and vulnerable lately, and she wanted someone on her side.

She'd also wanted him to kiss her, told herself she was wishing for it in an ephemeral,
shooting star sort of way. A wonderful, first
date kiss. Okay, second date. Third. A have-
your-cake-and-eat-it-too kiss. What made her
think she could just order it up? *I'll have one
of those with a little petting on the side.*

She felt like an idiot. Being tongue-tied was
probably a good thing. Whatever was on the
tip of it hadn't escaped. *I can't go to bed with
you, can't have sex with you, can't run away
with you.*

Nobody's asking you to, Celia.

And I certainly can't fall in love with you.

He'd get a good laugh out of that one. A
welcome laugh, no doubt. Nightmares left

people shaken, unbalanced and slightly cha-grined. A good laugh would have helped him throw all that off. She could have made him laugh by jumping from conclusion to conclu-sion like a kid playing in a trampoline park. Not that it was something she normally did anywhere but inside her head, but brightening a dark corner for a good man plagued with bad dreams seemed like a worthy cause. And Cougar wasn't the kind of man who would judge or take advantage or...

Damn. Was that a warning cramp? Celia slipped her hand under the elastic waistband of her pajama bottoms and rubbed her con-cave tummy. She wanted to slide her little finger lower very gradually, a fraction of an inch at a time, pick up where he'd left off, but she was feeling dangerously lightheaded, and her lips tingled. If she wasn't careful, she'd soon be giving birth to premature trust.

She awoke—surprised to be waking from what had surely been a night without sleep—to the sound of hammering somewhere outside. She looked at the clock, sprang from her bed and checked Mark's room. *No Mark.* She dashed to the kitchen and peeked through the yellow curtain on the back door toward the broken down corral.

Sigh of relief. Mark wielded the hammer while Cougar held a plank in place. Relief drew another breath and became full-blown delight. Mark was hammering! And Cougar was patiently supervising, helping him adjust his grip and strike the target.

Celia took a quick shower, put on a T-shirt

and a pair of jeans so that she could wear her boots, and dashed outside, her damp hair clipped high on the back of her head.

"Good morning," she chirped. Her glance ricocheted from Cougar's eyes, shaded by the brim of his hat, to her son, who didn't notice her. He was bent over a cinder block trying to tap the curve out of a bent nail. "You two are up early."

"Some of us are grateful to see the sun rise." His short-sleeved shirt was unbuttoned, and the sun was doing a glorious number on his bronze chest. "Coffee?"

"I haven't started it yet. I was surprised to see Mark out here. He's not supposed to leave the house without telling me. Did you…?"

"Nope. He came out to help. If I didn't know better, I'd've thought he heard the racket."

He gave her an enigmatic look as he reached around her for the blue plastic mug he'd left sitting on the wheel housing of his trailer. "Thought maybe you were ignoring us. I made coffee. Want some?"

"I'm sorry. I'll get breakfast—"

"Sorry about what?" He gestured with his coffee toward the camper door. "We had Lucky Charms. There's some left if you're interested."

"Sorry about the cold breakfast."

"It wasn't cold. It was just a little dry. But who needs milk when you've got Lucky Charms? Right, Mark?" It didn't seem to matter to him that Mark didn't look up. "This guy sure can swing a hammer."

"So can I." She glanced at the front end of the trailer. It would be interesting to find out how he liked his coffee. Even more interesting to see what was behind that door.

But she pivoted on her heel and turned her attention to her business. "What can I help with?"

"We're gonna need more nails." He nodded toward a collection of building supplies he'd gathered on a makeshift workbench fashioned from a pair of sawhorses and part of an old Dutch door. "That was the only box I found in the barn. I looked around pretty good."

She brightened. She had just what he needed. "There's a whole keg of them in the barn. An old wooden keg. It's probably been out there for fifty years or more."

"A nail is a nail." He nodded a come-on toward the trailer door. "What made you decide to buy a place like this?" he asked as he opened the door and gestured *after you.*

"Like what?" Stepping up on the running board, she glanced over her shoulder. "Rustic? Don't I strike you as the rustic type?"

"You don't strike me as a *type*." He smiled. "But you do strike me."

"And you do have coffee." And a tidy little kitchen with a tiny stove, sink, refrigerator, microwave, miniature cabinets that might have been part of a down-market trailer or an upscale playhouse. There were three books stacked on the bench seat—the top one written by Logan Wolf Track—and an iPod dock hanging on the wall. Music and books, she thought. Good signs.

"It's a good place." He was standing in the

doorway. "There's another cup above the sink. But you're pretty isolated."

"Not that far from Sinte, which is where I work, where Mark goes to school." She poured her coffee. "Is it okay if I nuke this?"

"Blast away. Sinte is pretty far from the beaten path," he noted. "People come to a reservation for a job, it's usually temporary. You buy a place like this, you're putting down roots."

"The price was right, and no one else wanted it." She pressed a button and smiled when the light came on in the little box above the stove. *So cute.* "My roots were tired of pots. They wanted solid ground. They like it here."

There was more to it, of course. She'd needed a place that was off the beaten path, but not so far off that she couldn't get Mark the help he needed. She thought she'd put the worst of her difficulties behind her. They could both sign the alphabet, even though Mark didn't seem interested in using it. Give him time, the specialists advised. Mark was still a mystery. She'd been able to keep him insured, and the Mayo Clinic, where he'd been treated originally, had recommended a good therapist for him in Rapid City. She hadn't expected Greg to follow her and insist on resuming his visitations with Mark after admitting he didn't know what to do with a kid who wasn't "normal."

But there was his lawsuit to consider.

"It's a good place," Cougar repeated as he backed away to let Celia out the door. "You can build on a place like this."

"The one thing I worry about is that Mark might be a little too isolated, especially when school's out. That's why I got started with the horse…" She squinted into the sunlight, shaded her eyes with her free hand and scanned the site. "Where did he go?"

"He went in the barn. He took me in and showed me around a while ago. He's the one who found the nails. Hey, what's the story on that old car back in the—"

"You asked him for nails?"

"I picked up the hammer, and he saw." He gave her a silly grin.

Cute again, but Cougar didn't get it. Working together was one thing, but Mark wasn't supposed to play in the barn alone. She set her coffee on the workbench and headed for the barn. "Celia," he called after her. But she kept going. First things first.

It took a moment for her eyes to adjust to the barn's murky shadows, but she heard a scraping sound, and when she saw what was making it, she stopped in her tracks. Mark was struggling with the nail keg.

"Cut him some slack," Cougar said quietly.

She turned, her heart pounding with excitement. "He *heard.*"

Cougar glanced past her toward Mark and then back again. He nodded, but when she started to speak, he signaled her to hold it. "Take a breath, Celia, you're scaring us." He smiled. "We've got nails."

She turned back to Mark. "Let me help you with that, Markie-B." She hoped to see his eyes before she touched him to get his attention, and she was disappointed when it didn't happen. In fact, he gave her a less-than-welcoming look when she laid hands on the keg. "No?"

"Mark's got it," Cougar said quietly. "We'll have ourselves a corral before dinnertime. I was just telling Mark before you came out, I can hardly wait to show him the Medicine Hat mustang. Told him the horse loaded pretty easy, which is a good sign."

She looked at him curiously.

"That's what *he* wanted to know. Sign of what? Sign that the horse is ready. Some signs speak louder than words."

"You think so?"

He thumbed his hat back. "'Course, I haven't written a *damn book* on the subject, but I know a thing or two about coming back from a wild place. It takes some adjustment."

"And you can't be sure who your friends are?" She watched as her son mastered rolling the heavy keg on the bottom rim. She felt rejected. Maybe she was the one who didn't get it.

"I think you know who your mother is. She's the one who's been there since day one. Mine's gone, but if she was still alive, I'd probably want to lean on her if she'd let me."

"Would she?"

"I don't know. It's been a long time. I like to think she would." He laid his hand on her shoulder. "For a little while. Maybe you don't want her to step back right away. But then something new comes along and you forget yourself for a few minutes. And then a few more and a few more."

"You're saying I'm too protective." Mark rolled the keg through the open door, set it down, looked up at her and grinned. She gave him a thumbs up. "So you don't think he *heard* you ask for nails."

"I'm saying he might just be listening more than you realize. I don't know if he's using his ears, but I think he's trying to hear and be heard." He slid his hand over her back and nudged her toward the door. "And I'm saying it'll be good to get this corral fixed so we can sneak over to Logan and Mary's place and try to load up the mustang without disturbing the honeymooners."

She nodded. "I see what you're saying."

"And seeing is one way to catch on. So you're good." He draped his forearm over her far shoulder. "Not fast, but good."

Chapter Six

There was no sneaking in and out at Logan and Mary Wolf Track's home. The couple was outside playing ground games with their claybank mustang with flashy black mane and tail. Logan had the horse batting a big rubber ball around the paddock with his muzzle, much to the delight of his wife, who had devoted her professional life to training dogs. The honeymooners were "in the zone," and

Mark fairly glowed as he watched. Any minute he's going to cheer, Celia told herself. She could almost hear his voice.

"Time out for substitutions," Mary called out. "Mama needs rest."

"Come on, Shoshoni, show us what you got." Logan patted the super-size beach ball and beckoned Cougar. "The name of the game is Horse's Pass."

"I just started the book," Cougar shouted. "Haven't gotten to that chapter yet? Are you in the pictures? 'Cause if this gets out, you won't make the Indian Cowboy Hall of Fame." But one look at the excitement in Mark's face had Cougar vaulting over the fence. He reached back over for Mark. "You and me, partner. What we've got is game."

"What would you like to drink?" Mary

asked Celia as they hiked themselves up on the open tailgate of Logan's pickup. Mary reached into a small cooler. "The choices are juice and water. And I have crackers and fruit. Try some strawberries." She offered up a pint box. "Please help me with these. It's like eating flavored packing peanuts, but don't tell Logan. He thinks he's getting me fresh fruit. He's forgotten what local fruit tastes like." She nodded toward the paddock, calling attention to the boys, the horse and their big red ball. "It looks like Cougar has a new tail."

"Simpatico," Celia mused as she bit into a nearly flavorless red and white strawberry. "I've never seen Mark take to anybody like this, especially after the accident."

"Logan said it started with a *near*-accident."

"No, I meant…"

Celia watched her son push the ball toward the horse, who whacked it right back and knocked the boy over like a bowling pin. She took a step toward the fence, but Mark came up grinning, and the words *it started* hit her between the eyes. *The accident* did not refer to the same seminal event for everybody.

"Well, yes," she amended, "Mark ran out in front of Cougar's pickup. He was chasing a cat. Cougar's pickup sits up so high, he didn't see him, but somehow he stopped the truck in time. It was pretty miraculous, actually."

"It was Cougar. That sixth sense of his has saved a few lives, including his own." Mary tossed half a strawberry into the grass and reached into the cooler without taking her eyes away from the game. "That is one brave cowboy."

"He said he spent some time in a VA hospital." Celia reached into the cooler for a cold bottle of cranberry juice. "I know he's struggling with his own demons. He doesn't need Mark's."

"Oh, but he'll gladly take them on. He's been decorated, too. One medal he has that I don't want is a Purple Heart."

"What…I mean, can you tell what me happened?"

"There was an explosion," Mary said on the tail-end of a swallow of orange juice. She sounded matter-of-fact, as though she were reporting a fireworks display.

"One of those roadside IEDs?"

"Improvised explosive device," Mary mused. "It sounds almost clinical, doesn't it? It's the improvised part, the creativity that makes things interesting. Each one is unique."

Celia studied the label on the juice bottle—an upended crate with a scattering of red fruit. "I haven't asked him for details."

"Neither have I, but I've read the report." Mary leaned forward, elbows braced on her thighs, juice bottle cradled in both hands in the chasm between her knees. "Some of my dog handlers were in Cougar's unit. An incident report can read pretty dry, too, kinda what it might be like to read a movie script, you know? This character moves here, this vehicle comes in over there."

Cougar called for "heads up," and he play-tackled Mark, swept him off the ground and swung him around, slinging him over his shoulder like a sack of meal. The game had apparently been called with the ball in the mustang's corner. Grinning, Mark swiped Cougar's cowboy hat and put it on his own head.

Mary sipped her orange juice. "What looked like a couple with two kids crossed their truck's path. Cougar was driving. He saw that something didn't look right, but he slowed down anyway because one of the kids lost this goat he was dragging along behind him.

"Long story short, Cougar suddenly thought he was riding a cutting horse. He used the truck to cut the kid out of the little pack, and then he jumped out and called to the woman to send him the other kid. Somehow he knew the woman was wired and the kids were being used to keep her in line. She exploded, and the child close to her was killed. Cougar caught some shrapnel. The goat and its little herder were okay. It was an up-armored truck, and it was far enough from the explosion—thanks to Cougar—that nobody else was injured."

Logan served the ball over the fence volleyball-style. It bounced to within a few feet of the women's dangling boots. "What are you drinking?" he shouted to his wife.

"Sunshine." She held the bottle aloft, and he gave a thumbs-up.

Sunshine. Sergeant Mary Tutan Wolf Track was filling up on sunshine in the wake of living with long, dark stories made short for eyes and ears on the home front. Celia imagined witnessing an explosion of human beings. Unimaginable, yes, but her mind's eye came up with a picture that was clearer than her memory of her son lying face down in a pool of blood. In her head she could see through Cougar's eyes, but not her own. Her mind protected her from her memory.

"What about the man?" Celia asked Mary quietly. "You said it was a couple."

"I said it *looked like* a couple. The man got away. Apparently lived to fight another day."

"Oh, God, how is that fair?"

"Only God knows, I guess." The men were on the move from paddock to pen, where Cougar's Paint gelding eyed them warily. "Cougar's a good man who's had a rough time. But I can't think of anyone I'd rather have in my foxhole except one of my dogs."

"What about Logan?"

"Logan?" Mary grinned. "He'd be too much of a distraction. Stay alert, stay alive."

"No kidding." Celia drew a deep breath. "How serious were Cougar's injuries?"

"That's for him to say." Mary shut down for a moment, and they both watched as Logan approached the mustang while Cougar and Mark stood back and let the "master" work his magic.

Wrong question. Celia's face felt flush. She'd overstepped, and she'd gotten some push-back. She wanted to bite her tongue.

Mary smiled wistfully. "He looks a lot better than he did the last time I saw him, I'll say that much."

"We haven't known him long, but that doesn't seem to matter. I mean, we've both really…" She was watching Logan and Cougar prepare to load the mustang in Cougar's trailer. He'd made sure Mark was safely out of the way but well within view of the activity.

"Taken to him?"

"I guess you could say that. The thing is…" She tried to remember the last time her son had seemed at once connected to what was going on around him and carefree. "Mark doesn't need any more demons, either."

"From what I understand, neither do you."

Celia glanced warily at her new friend wondering what she'd heard, and from whom, and what she thought about it. With a challenging new job, new friends, dramatically different surroundings, she had hoped to make a new life for herself. She'd spent way too much energy trying to keep up appearances over the years. She wanted to be done with that, to revive the simple what-you-see-is-what-you-get kind of a girl she'd once been. But something inside her jumped up and down shouting, *Oh, no, we're fine.*

Her demons had always ridden pogo sticks.

And that image made her laugh, which allowed her to nod in agreement. "But what're ya gonna do?" she quipped. "No demons, no angels."

"I like that one. Do you mind if I add it to my book of mottos?"

"Be my guest. I'm appropriating, *Stay alert, stay alive.*"

"Be careful with that one. If you're drinking Red Bull and popping pills to stay awake so you don't get killed, you've gotten yourself into some seriously unfriendly territory."

"Shouldn't have to live that way," Celia said soberly.

"Shouldn't," Mary agreed.

"Did you see that?" Cougar called out, turning both women's heads. The three guys were standing beside open trailer doors. Cougar gave a sweeping gesture. "He loaded right up." He laid his hand on Mark's shoulder and gave an affectionate squeeze. "We're on our way, partner."

Mark looked up, grinning to beat the band. "Right?"

Mark nodded. Celia's breath got hung up in her chest. Understanding a one-word question without hearing it was not such a big deal, but Mark's ready response was remarkable.

Don't jump all over it, Celia. Let the turtle feel the sun on his face.

"So you're partners now." She greeted Mark with a mother's unconscious reach for the mat of damp hair on the sweaty forehead, which Mark ducked for the first time ever. *Give me a break, Mom. I'm not a baby.*

"Oh, yeah," Cougar said. "We're a team. We're rescuing horses and houses, giving each cause equal time—half the day training, the other half fixing up. We're gonna be busy."

"Mark's going to be in summer school camp next week."

"Summer school *camp?* That sounds cool." Cougar was sorting through the bottles in the cooler, assessing the choices. "What kind of school does he go to?"

"He goes to school in Sinte. I hope I never have to send him away to school. I hope…" She watched Cougar exchange signals with Mark. *How about some water? Catch.* So clear. So easy. So natural. "They're trying something new with his group this summer. The kids sign up for a week at a time, so they can take time off or hang in there the whole summer. And it's fun. It's like camp, but with the three R's deftly woven in."

"His group?" Cougar swallowed half a bottle of water in one gulp and then gave her a look that said, *I'm listening.*

"Special needs."

"Well, we'll weave in two more R's—ridin' and ropin'." He grinned at the sight of Mark gulping down his water. "Oh, man, I went to summer school *wishing* I could go to camp. Then I went to boot camp and wished I was back in school. This guy already knows how to put his horse in front of the cart.

Right, partner?" They shared an enthusiastic high-five.

"You boys are gonna do fine with that horse," Logan put in as he took his turn at the drinks box. "You got a name for him?"

"Mark's gonna name him. Soon as he comes up with just the right one, he'll tell me." Cougar tapped Logan's arm with the back of his drinking hand. "Hey, we'll have a naming ceremony."

"You know, Mark can write," Celia said. "He won't always do it for me, but he does it in school all the time."

"He won't pass notes to you?" Cougar laughed. "I'll teach him how to pass notes. I was always pretty good at stuff like that."

"I'll bet you were," Celia said with a smile.

We're a team, he'd said. Her son was on a team.

"I don't know much about special needs, but Mark has special gifts."

"I know he does." Celia lifted one shoulder. "But I'm a bit biased."

"I'm not, so you can take my word." He waited for her eyes to connect with his, and when they did, he nodded. "And do whatever you want with it."

Somewhere in the periphery, Logan said to his wife, "I don't think he's coming back to our place anytime soon, do you?"

Cougar laughed. "Like I said, I appreciate the offer, but Celia's got some work for me to do."

"My place needs a lot of work," Celia explained to Mary. "I bought the old Krueger place a few months ago. West of here about ten miles. Do you know it?"

Mary nodded. "How long was that place empty?"

"Long enough to bring the price down to within a teacher's reach. The house has good bones with deteriorating flesh and peeling skin."

Cougar tapped Mary's arm with the back of his hand. "I've got a few skills you don't know about, First Sergeant Tutan."

"I'll bet you do, Staff Sergeant Cougar. I'm glad you're putting them to use." She smiled wistfully. "I'm leaving tomorrow. Next time I see you, I'll be wearing civvies twenty-four seven." She rolled her eyes heavenward. "If all goes well."

"Hey, you tell them they'll still be able to

get Tutan-trained dogs," Cougar said. "They show you the money, you'll show them the contract. Hell, everyone else is doing it."

Mary laid her hand on her belly. "Before long I'm going to be showing more than a contract."

"Congratulations," Cougar said, and Celia chimed in with, "That's wonderful."

"Which might have been reason enough to stay in the army a while longer, but…" She glanced at her husband. "Did I tell you I qualified for post-separation delivery?"

Logan jacked up one eyebrow. "Meaning?"

"I can have the baby on Uncle Sam's dime." She smiled. "Because I'm worth it."

At the sound of his horse getting restless in the trailer, Cougar offered Mary a handshake. "Stay safe."

"Stay *here,* Cougar. You have friends here."

He laughed. "You don't think I have friends in other places?"

"Not like these two. It's hard to come back to the same old stuff. It looks like what you've always called home, but it feels different. And it's not because it *is* different. It's because *you're* different, and they haven't changed."

Cougar gave a dry chuckle. "Ain't that the truth."

The rubber had barely met the blacktop before Mark was fast asleep in the backseat of Cougar's pickup. He'd had a good day. Celia was smiling as she turned back around in her seat, catching a glimpse of the man at the wheel. She loved that cowboy hat, which was amazing. *A cowboy hat?* It wasn't a costume. It was Cougar. She tried to imagine him wearing a uniform, and the image wouldn't take form. The hat, the shirt, the jeans, the boots, they were Cougar.

He glanced at her. "Sounds like Sergeant Tutan's all wound up. Did she give you an earful?"

"Not quite. There's room left if you want to add more."

He nodded, intent on the road ahead. "This is where I'm supposed to say something like, I've done some bad stuff, war's hell and I can't talk about it. But trust me. I'm one of the good guys."

"If that's what you're saying, I believe you."

He glanced at her again. "Which part?"

"It all sounds true." She smiled. "My son has good instincts, and he trusts you."

"What about you?"

"I like you very much, Cougar. I think you know that. As for my instincts, they're still on probation."

Mark was dying to get down off the fence and get up close and personal with the horse with no name. Cougar was doing his damnedest to concentrate on keeping the horse moving about the pen—he'd lose the horse the minute he lost his focus—while he kept the boy in the periphery of his field of vision. His training served him well. Mark's enthusiasm was palpable, and he felt good about that.

No Name was aware of it, too. He knew Mark was his kind. Speechless and sensitive, the two would connect when the time came, and Cougar looked forward to seeing it happen. What animal didn't have special needs?

Especially the young ones. Make a safe place for them, let them stretch their legs and test their senses while you chase the vultures away and pick off the poachers.

He would have welcomed the sound of an approaching vehicle had it been a small car instead of a noisy panel truck. *Bread and Butter Bakery*. Celia hadn't said anything about Greg Banyon possibly stopping in while she was doing her errands, so this must have been somebody's unexpected pleasure. Cougar couldn't imagine whose.

Banyon parked close to the corral, but he didn't get out of the truck. Instead he hung his head out the window and shouted at Mark. "How's my boy?"

Cougar could see him through the fence. The odd salute he affected didn't merit a response. "You gonna teach him to ride?" Banyon shouted as he emerged from the truck.

"This is a mustang," Cougar said. "We're gentling him."

"That's a wild horse? Mark, get down off that fence!" Banyon lunged for the fence, shouting the boy's name. He got a piece of Mark's T-shirt, but it slipped though his fingers as Mark fell or jumped—Cougar wasn't sure which—into the pen. The horse's ears flattened, and he started dancing back and forth on the opposite side. Cougar stood between the boy and the nervous animal.

"Jesus," Cougar muttered. He backed into Mark's corner quickly, picked him up and set him on his feet, keeping his eyes on the mustang. "It's okay, Mark. You're okay."

"What the hell is wrong with you?" Banyon yelled. "That's a wild animal."

"Meaning what?" Cougar shepherded Mark over the fence. "He's liable to do something crazy?"

"You've got a wild horse and a deaf mute child here," Banyon ranted. "I was trying to grab him down, get him out of harm's way." He eyed the boy, who wasn't going near him, and then the horse, who was taking the same precaution. "What's going on here, anyway? She's bringing those wild mustangs over *here* now?"

Cougar pulled on his fireproof suit, covered himself with calm. "Celia isn't here right now. Was she expecting you?"

Banyon looked befuddled, thrown off course. "I...I tried calling. Got no answer, so…so I thought I'd stop on my way by. Where is she?"

"She had some business to do."

Banyon's eyes narrowed. "And she left my son with you?"

He was back on course.

"Mark wanted to stay. I don't know if it's me or the horse, but at least one of us must be pretty interesting."

Banyon humphed, turning his attention to a car passing on the highway. "When do you expect Cecilia back?"

Cougar's calm was waning. He needed to keep quiet, keep the last of it from draining away.

"Did you hear me? I said, *when…*" Banyon stepped back as reality suddenly hit him between the eyes. He lowered his voice, but he couldn't quite bring himself to drop the bluster. "I had some news for her. Now I *really* have news for her. She can't go off and leave him with just anyone." He shrugged. "No offense, but we don't know you."

When they say no offense, you know the offense is incoming. Just stay cool. Let it drop on the ground and roll away.

Cougar laughed. Dr. Choi knew the triggers.

"Look, we're not putting on a show here." Cougar gave Mark's shoulder a soft squeeze to let him know he hadn't forgotten where the boy stood. "If you want to watch, why don't you sit in your truck?"

"I gotta get back to work, and I should be taking Mark with me." But he moved in the direction Cougar suggested. "I'm gonna trust you this time." He pointed at Cougar and then toward the corral. "But don't let him near that horse. That's one of the things his mother's been doing without my approval. Being around those wild horses." He jerked the door open on his truck with one hand, leaving the other free for more pointing. "You tell her I stopped by. Tell her she'd better pick up when I call."

Cougar could feel the tension melt from Mark's shoulders as they watched the truck speed away, leaving a dust wake in the air and a bitter taste in the mouth. He steered Mark back to the fence and helped him climb up and straddle the top rail. They watched the mustang regain his balance. His ears rotated, testing out the vibes.

"I'd like for you to name him for me," Cougar said as they watched. He didn't think of it as talking to himself. Just planting seeds. "You don't have to come up with anything right now, but just be thinking about it. Let me know when it comes to you."

Mark unsnapped the flap on the big pocket of his cargo pants, reached in and pulled out a toy airplane. Cougar looked him in the eye, letting him know he was all ears and then some. The boy showed him the name on the side of the fuselage.

Flyboy.

Cougar swallowed hard and nodded slowly. There was no doubt.

"That's a good name. We'll try it out on him and see if he likes it." He smiled. *Not too big. Not too scary. Let him pace himself.* "Your mom says you get to go to summer camp pretty soon. Do they ride horses at this camp?"

Mark rubbed the word *Flyboy* with his forefinger.

"I'm guessing that means no, so we'll have our own camp here. You get your own personal trainer. You and Flyboy."

Cougar drew a deep breath. *Keep talking. You're giving no offense, and something's getting through.*

"I didn't have horses at my camp, either. Plenty of guns, but no horses. I was a soldier. I wanted to be a warrior, you know? Defend the people. Whoever's getting pushed around." He patted Mark's knobby knee. "Anybody tries to push you around, you've got Cougar to back you. That's my last name, Cougar.

"In the Army you get a nametag with just

your last name, so the day I put on that uniform, I stopped using any other name. Why would anyone name her kid Calvin Cougar, huh?" He touched his finger to his lips. "That's just between you and me, okay? Don't tell anybody. I guess Cal ain't such a bad handle, but when you have a name like Cougar, why use anything else?

"You know what a cougar is? They live around here, out in the hills. They're wild." He gave an expansive gesture. The boy was with him. He was sure of it. "Ever been to a zoo? You don't wanna see a cougar in a zoo. It makes you wanna puke."

And you don't want to be a Cougar in a cage. It makes you wanna kill the guy who put you there.

"Flyboy's checking us out. See his eyes?"

Cougar pointed, and Mark followed his finger. "Watch his ears. He's got his own radar, like they have at airfields. He'll learn to trust us. No other horses around, so we're all he's..." The sound of a little four-banger engine drew Cougar's head around. "Hey, your mom's back."

He'd been engrossed in his therapy session. He wasn't sure who was getting more out of it, but Cougar must've been heavily invested if Celia's car could reach the yard without raising either defenses or anticipation.

He jumped down from the fence and reached for Mark. "Should we tell her? You know, about your dad." Mark gave him a funny look. "Yeah, you're right. Mind your own business, Cougar."

They sauntered over to the little blue car

like a pair of watchmen checking out a visitor. But when Celia emerged, both faces brightened.

"Hey," Cougar said.

"Hey." She looked at him curiously, as though she thought he might be up to something. And she expected to be pleasantly surprised.

"We have something to show you." It wasn't much, but it would do. He took her by the hand and signaled Mark to lead the way to the corral, where they showed her the plywood hay feeder they'd built. He nodded toward the far side of the pen. "It's going in that corner. Got the water hooked up so we don't have to haul it by the bucket."

"So you got the pump...Mark?"

He'd crawled through the newly repaired fence.

Cougar scaled the fence and started to intervene, but Mark took two steps and stood quietly. The horse stood just as quietly.

"Cou—"

Cougar signaled Celia to be still.

The horse lowered his head and took one step. Mark made a quarter turn and started walking away from the Paint the way he'd seen Cougar do earlier with little success. Muzzle near the ground, the horse followed.

"I'll be damned," Cougar whispered.

Mark glanced at Cougar first, and then his mom. He was all smiles.

"Mark named him Flyboy," Cougar said as he unloaded a couple of cloth grocery bags and a cooler on Celia's kitchen counter. Mark grabbed a small box out of the way and took it to the kitchen table.

Celia looked up from ditching her shoes just inside the back door. "Mark did?"

"The name's written on the side of one of his planes. He showed it to me." Mark was pulling more planes out of the box, seemingly oblivious to what was being said about him. The excitement of his moment with the horse had apparently passed. Cougar felt a little deflated.

"And you decided to use it. He'd like that."

Cougar nodded. He was damn sure the kid tipped his hand over the name. Whether Mark knew what he was doing was another question. Whether he was even *doing* what he was doing. He glanced at Mark, lining several plastic planes up for takeoff. If he heard what was being said, he wasn't responding.

If he heard what was being said, he had amazing control.

Cougar would tell her and let her judge for herself. But not yet. He wasn't sure whether Mark had in his own way confided in Cougar, and if he had, he wasn't sure what the boy really wanted him to do with the information. Or maybe Mark didn't know, either, and they were both feeling their way along.

"How about I take you guys out to supper?" Cougar suggested impulsively.

"How about I make us some supper?" Celia laid her hand on his arm. "I want to."

"After I earn it," he insisted. "I haven't started on the deck yet."

"You fixed the corral."

"I needed to use it. That's not something you… Hey, you never told me about that old car in the back of the barn."

"Like the rest of that stuff, it came with the barn," she said. "Do you fix cars, too? If you do, you're welcome to it. I have no use—"

"Not so fast, woman. You don't just give away a sixty-six Ford Fairlane."

"I don't even know if it has an engine. It's probably home to colonies of—"

"It's clean." He shrugged, a little embarrassed about nosing around. "I checked. It's a car covered with tarp, what can I say?"

She laughed. "Say you'll stay out of my closet."

"Hell, I'm a man. I don't care what's in your closet." He grinned. "But you've got potential muscle in your barn."

"So you're a car man."

"I'm a horse man," he averred. "But my brother, Eddie, he's crazy about cars."

"So there's a brother," she said as though she'd just bought herself a clue.

"Now who's diggin' around in the closet?"

"We'll talk about the car and the deck over supper. It's been ages since I made my special lasagna." She gave him a teasing glance. "Unless you're worried we might be buttering you up."

"I like butter. How much butter do you serve with your lasagna?"

"As much as you want. I didn't get any bread at the store because I'm not a fan of their bakery, but…" She waggled her delicate eyebrows. "I prefer to bake my own.

And I don't have to ask how homemade bread sounds. You're a man."

"You got that right. I'm definitely a man." He smiled wistfully. "And I'd be lying if I said I don't know what I'm doing here. I like it here, and I don't want to wear out my welcome. I keep wanting to see you again, and this way...by helping out..."

"I know what you mean."

"No, you don't," he said quietly. It felt as though they'd known each other a while because they'd hit it off right away, but he had stuff in his closet he didn't want dragged out. He'd barely managed to get the door closed on it. He'd figured on traveling around with it for a while, letting it settle after all the wrestling around he'd done with it.

He looked into her eyes. "You don't know

anything about the man who wants to see you again."

"Yes, I do. I trust you, Cougar."

"I don't. I have too many raw places, Celia." He glanced at Mark, whose planes were lined up by size, and the smallest one was taxiing toward the end of the table. "I came here looking for a simple connection. I know horses. I *love* horses. These horses, there's still that wildness in them, but it's natural. The wildness in me is…" His eyes connected with hers again. Not the connection he'd been looking for, but the one he'd be hard-pressed to walk away from now. "I don't know what to do about it. I thought the horse could teach me."

"Mary told me a little bit about the incident that put you in the hospital. Only the official report. She said the rest was up to you." She laid her hand over the back of his. "I know you saved lives. How can you not trust a man who would risk his life for someone he didn't—"

"It wasn't like that." He wasn't claiming any heroics, and he didn't want anyone else doing it in his behalf. "I didn't think about it. I acted. After something like that happens, *then* you get to thinkin' about it. There were other people in my truck. I don't know what would have happened if I'd just floored the damn thing like I was trained to do. Maybe what I really did was I set the guy off. I acted, and he reacted."

"What do you think would have happened?"

"All the thinking I do now ain't worth..." He shook his head as he slid his hand out from under hers. "But I do it anyway. I think about it, and I dream about it, and here I am talking about it." It was his turn to claim her hand. No sympathy. No seduction. "I just want to see you again. I want to be a normal guy who meets a woman, likes her right away, she likes him and they can go on seeing each other and find out where it takes them."

"If I make lasagna, will you have supper with us? Because I'm not going to make that recipe if I'm going to be eating leftovers for a week."

"I'm gonna start on the deck tomorrow." Mark looked up from his toys. *"We,"* Cougar amended. "My partner and I will get started tomorrow."

Chapter Seven

After the supper dishes were done, Cougar took a few measurements on the deck while Celia put Mark to bed. Through an open window he could hear her reading a story about an owl, which creeped him out some since having an owl stay near the house all night was a bad sign for an Indian, and telling owl stories might draw them in. An owl could hear a mouse step on a blade of grass. But he didn't give away his position. He just sat there and took it all in, much the way Mark did, waiting for the right time. Time for the owl to attack, time for Mark to...

He wasn't sure what Mark was waiting for. Perimeter security, maybe. He was staying inside until somebody secured the perimeter.

Security was Cougar's specialty. Hell, he'd been an MP for ten years. Protect and defend. *We take care of our own.* He could do that, no problem. He'd thought about looking for a job as a cop. They'd want to train him a little differently, and they'd find him to be a quick study.

But his medical records would be a quick study, too. Combat-related disability. Most people didn't know what to make of post-traumatic stress disorder. Was it safe to be around him? He didn't know for sure. He'd scared himself a few times. Heavy-duty meds had become part of the problem, so he was weaning himself off, trying to clear the cobwebs, and he was almost there. But the dreams were back. And the dreams were deadly.

"That didn't take long," Celia announced as she emerged from the house. "He was tired. You must've kept him busy while I was gone. Or was it the other way around?"

"We're a team." Down on one knee, Cougar dropped the tape measure into his toolbox and closed the lid. "We have a connection. It's hard to explain, but…" He stared out into the night, toward the corral. "The horse is in on it, too. The connection. The therapy program I was in…" Damn. Nobody was asking for an explanation. He needed to take a cue from Mark and keep his damn mouth shut. He flipped the latch on the toolbox. "You know, they used horses."

She was quiet. He stood up, tucked his hands in his back pockets, felt a little awkward. Fits and starts, he thought. He wasn't a big talker, but when he was with Celia, it was easy to *start* saying whatever was on his mind, which didn't really *fit* with who he was, where he was or what he was doing there. But it felt okay until his mind caught up with his mouth.

Don't go there. Not now.

"I couldn't find anything like that for Mark," she said finally. "But I've read a lot about therapy with animals, especially horses, and I know that volunteering at the sanctuary has helped us both." She held her hand out to him. "Walk with me?"

Her hand felt small and cool in his. She set the pace for slow and the course for meandering. A warm breeze discouraged mosquitoes, and the enormous sky provided enough starlight and moonlight to cast across their path the shadowy shape of a couple joined at the hip and sliding along the grass.

"You think he'll wake up and be scared?" Cougar asked.

"He'll sleep soundly. If he gets up, it's usually not until two or three o'clock in the morning."

"Yeah, that's about the right time for a nightmare." They were wandering in the direction of the corral. "You said there's no physical reason for him not to be able to hear."

"That's what the doctors say. They've done all kinds of testing."

"I'm gonna go out on a limb and tell you he heard me when I asked him to come up with a name for the horse."

She stopped and turned to him. "Are you sure?"

"He had to. He wasn't watching me, couldn't have read my lips. And that's not the only time." He cradled her hand in both of his. "He's protecting himself, Celia."

"From me?"

"I don't know what's in his mind. I know I've got some scary stuff in mine."

"That could be part of the connection between you." She sighed. "But I have some of that, too. Not the real pain, but the…" She covered her stomach with her free hand. "Phantom pain, I guess."

Cougar nodded. "He doesn't have much connection with his father."

"His father thinks Mark is a potential cash cow." She groaned. "That sounds awful."

"He stopped by here today. He doesn't like me much, and the feeling is mutual. I get the feeling he's looking for ammunition he can fire off at you, and I look like a possibility."

"What did he want?"

"Said he had some news for you."

She sighed. "It's always about that damn lawsuit. You know how long those things can drag on? If it wasn't for that, he'd leave us alone."

"You're not on board with it?"

"I'm not going to sit around counting chickens. Mark's medical needs are covered, along with any therapy or training or special needs relating to his injuries. If anything comes of these other claims, the lawyer will get a big chunk of it."

"The man doesn't think you should leave Mark with me." He drew her hand around the back of his waist, put his arm around her shoulders, and started them moving again. "You don't know me well enough."

"Where have I heard that before?" She gave his waist a quick squeeze. "My only worry is that I might be taking advantage of you. Not that I would ask you to…"

"You didn't. I offered. Mark…"

"…wanted to stay with you today. I know a lot about you, Cougar." She looked up at him, offering a moonlit smile. "Except your name. I'm pretty sure there's more to it."

He returned her smile by half. "Cougar isn't enough for you?"

They'd reached the corral, where Flyboy stood hipshot, probably wondering why he wasn't walking around in the grass with his new herd.

Celia turned to Cougar. "Not when there's more to it. I want the whole story."

"Why?" He traced the curve of her chin with his thumb. "Take my word, it ain't gonna get any better than Cougar."

"Be careful. I don't take words lightly." But she took his hips lightly in her hands, tucking her thumbs in his belt. "That was a pretty big deal, wasn't it? For the horse to follow Mark the way he did?"

"It was beautiful, but don't weigh it or measure it. Just take it to heart."

"Mark spoke to him, didn't he? Somehow they spoke to each other."

He reached for her hands as though he were drawing six-shooters from his holsters. But rather than aim and shoot, he lifted each one in turn to his lips. "I don't want my being here to bring any trouble down on you."

"You're not... You mean from Greg? No." She squeezed his hands. "No, he can't..." She shook her head. "No. We're past that."

"Sounds like there's more to the story."

She released his hands, and he turned toward the corral, leaned back against the pickup, separating himself but standing right beside her. Her sentry.

She drew breath, as though she were about

to go under for a while, but she let it out quickly, and she spoke quietly.

"I used to think jealousy was a sign of...I don't know, love, I guess. I took it lightly. It was high school stuff, kind of sweet. But then we had Mark, and we weren't kids anymore. We were both supposed to be parents." She gave a dry chuckle. "Greg was jealous."

"Of Mark?"

"Of anybody that wasn't Greg. He was always suspicious, always checking up on me. We tried to fix things. I mean...well, we got some counseling." She shook her head. "After Mark's accident, there was nothing left. Mark needed attention, and Greg couldn't deal with any of it. But he couldn't leave us alone, either. Especially after he got started on *his son's lawsuit*." She looked up at him. "I'm sorry for…if he said anything insulting. I want you to stay, Cougar, but I'll certainly understand…"

"He's not gonna run me off."

"Good."

"I don't wanna get into it with him, so I'll try to steer clear. But if you need me, you say the word."

"What word would that be?"

"Cougar." He toyed with a wisp of her hair escaped from the clip that had the rest trapped. "Just don't use it lightly."

"Are you a lethal weapon?"

"I can be." His finger lifted the strand of hair, traced the curve of her ear and, joined by three more fingers, made a path toward the back of her head. "But I'm learning how to turn it down a notch."

"A notch below lethal?"

"I just need more practice." He smiled as he released the clip and sprang her hair loose.

"The word is *Cougar*."

He turned to her again, sank his fingers into her hair and held her head in his hands, took his time parting his lips as she prepared for him by moistening hers. His mouth hovered until he felt her breath on his face, and he drew it in quickly, touching his tongue to her lower lip as she lifted herself to him. He claimed his kiss fully, held her head, rubbed her hair between his fingers, pressed his hips close, but not tight. Not yet. He was well below lethal. Plenty of room to maneuver.

He backed off, kissed her softly, flirted with her tongue, let his hands drift over her shoulders, his thumb brush her nape and discover the down that must have covered her head when she was a baby.

"Cougar," she whispered, and this time the sound of his name borne on her breath sent a shock wave deep into his belly.

"Careful." He shifted his legs apart, gathered her close, kissed her just beneath her ear and whispered in a way meant to warm her and make her shiver in the same instant. "Careful, careful."

"I don't say it lightly."

"Yes, you do." He slipped his hands under her T-shirt and slid them up her back. From the small of her back to her shoulder blades, nothing but soft skin over firm muscle. She put her arms around his neck, and his thumbs brushed the outer fullness of her breasts. "You make it float," he whispered into her hair.

She turned her face to him, nuzzled his ear, nipped his lobe and made a soft, sweet sound deep in her throat when his thumbs edged close to her nipples. He rocked his hips against hers. Damn, his jeans were getting tight. She took the lead on the next kiss, slipped him some tongue and took his hungrily when her turn came. Her nipples had beaded up even before he touched them.

He rested his forehead on hers and fought to contain himself long enough to ask, "Do you want to go inside?"

"No." She buried her fingers in his hair. "Because I can't take you with me."

"My camper is closer."

"I can't." But she kissed him as though she could, and then she said, "Step by step, Cougar. You're making *me* float."

"I've barely started."

"I know." She hugged his neck and whispered in his ear. "Not so fast, cowboy."

Celia and Mark stood at the end of their dirt road under the puffy blue and red umbrella of a morning sky. During the school year Mark rode to school with Celia, and she'd been leery of letting him ride the bus to summer school, but the program director had urged her to give it a try. The first few times had been a little iffy—not for Mark as much as for Celia—but now she felt good about putting him on the bus. He was stretching out those baby steps, and she was keeping hands off, feet still, eyes on her precious prize.

The bus door folded open, and the driver

greeted them with his usual report. "We're finally gonna get some rain today, looks like."

"We'll see," said aide Vicky Long Soldier, appearing at the top of the steps. "Merle makes the same prediction every day. He's bound to get it right eventually." She descended the steps slightly sideways, owing to sore knees and extra pounds. She'd assisted in special education through a parade of teachers with younger knees and impressive degrees, and she was still going strong. "Right, Mark? Are you ready to go on a field trip today?"

Mark looked up at his mother. *Do I have to go?*

"There'll be plenty of time for you to work with Cougar when you get back. He'll have

Flyboy ready and waiting." *Show me you understand. Give me a sign.*

"You have a cougar and a flyboy?" Vicky extended her hand to Mark. "I can't wait to see what that's all about." She glanced at Celia. "He might write something about it. I know he'll draw me something."

Flashing a smile over his shoulder, Mark took Vicky's hand. He was suddenly fine with something that was happening. Maybe something he'd heard. Celia glanced at the always magnificent, ever intimidating sky. Change was in the air.

"Call me if he needs me to come get him." Celia gave a wan smile. "For any reason."

"He's doing good. We're going to see alpacas and llamas today."

"We visited that farm once. Mark loved it.

They also raise rabbits." She remembered Mark's reluctance to surrender the baby bunny he'd been allowed to hold, and she reached out impulsively. "Don't let him—"

"Don't worry," Vicky called out as she slid into the seat behind the driver. "Nobody rides a llama without a helmet."

Celia smiled as she watched the bus head back down the road. She had a feeling Mark was on the verge of a breakthrough. Granted, it wasn't a new feeling, but it was gaining strength. Mark was going to be okay.

And Celia was finding her way. For a woman whose carefully planned household had unraveled quickly once the first thread was pulled, she'd been feeling pretty good lately about boldly choosing the road less traveled and sticking to the path. Even when Greg had shown up, she reminded herself that she was there first. And when Cougar had shown up, she'd had no expectations, and she'd discovered that surprises could be pleasant. Waking up in the morning to the sound of demolition didn't seem so great at first, but when she looked at the clock, she'd been grateful for the wake-up call, along with the sound of a man keeping his promise.

He hadn't seemed to notice her moving around in the kitchen, and she felt oddly shy about bouncing outside to greet him first thing, so she'd made coffee and hustled Mark down to the bus stop. Back in the house she saw no sign that he'd helped himself, so she filled a cup with coffee and opened the back door in time to watch him heave a tattered plank off the deck. He turned, ready to grab another one. His expression softened, business to pleasure, and he greeted her with a cowboy salute—the touch of a finger to the brim of a hat—a little different from the crisp salute he'd given Mary on the heels of paying her public tribute, but offered with equal ease by the same man.

One look and she was ready to leap.

"Whoa!" The salute became a warning flag. He pointed toward the hole she was about to put her foot in.

"That's your second save this morning." She doubled the stretch in her step-off leg and flip-flopped over to his side of what was left of the deck. "I forgot to set the alarm, so your racket was timely." She handed him the coffee. "Mark made it to the bus."

"You might want to use the front door for a

couple of days, especially after it rains." He cast a glance overhead as he sipped.

"That's two rain forecasts. You and the bus driver." She scanned the sky. "Those don't look like rain clouds."

"They aren't. They're warnings. Put them together with the barometer in my head, and you've got a sure thing."

"You have an imaginary barometer?" Under his hat, buried in his beautiful black hair. She smiled at the image.

"Oh, it's real. Got one in my head and one in my back."

"Cougar, you don't have to do this now. You don't have to do it at all."

He handed her the coffee and bent to pick up another splintered plank.

"Cougar!"

He tossed the plank into the grass and turned with a tight smile. "Okay, now's the time to use words lightly. The headache is down to a dull roar, and I'd like to keep it that way."

"But you don't have to—"

"I want to. Actually, I *need* to. I've learned the hard way. I give myself an injection, and I keep moving. I don't think about it until I realize, hey, it's almost gone."

"Can I help?"

"Sure, if you put some shoes on." He took the coffee back and ushered her to the edge of the deck, where he motioned for her to take a seat with his red toolbox between them. He pulled out two pieces of paper. "I have two plans, A and B.

"I started out with Plan B, and then I started

dreaming up options. See?" He pushed the toolbox aside and sidled closer, presenting his drawings as though he actually had a stake in all this—a grade, a medal, a check, something more than parking space. "Plan A has some extra cool stuff. Two satellite decks. This one's a play area for Mark, and this one's for stargazing." He pointed out each part of the pencil drawing, neatly executed with a straight edge. "And then up here, you can have this workbench for whatever project you've got going. I see you do some gardening, and you build little things and decorate stuff."

He pointed to a cross-hatched area. "I wanna put up some shade here and here. Build a frame and maybe throw some cottonwood cuttings on to start with."

"Like a bowery," she enthused.

"To start," he stressed, as though she might take exception to the lovely traditional touch. "You and Mark are both pretty pale until you turn pink for a day or two, and then it's back to pale."

"Peel first. Then back to pale."

"I wasn't gonna mention that, but, yeah. I read that you people get a lot of skin cancer out here on the prairie." He gave her a lop-sided smile. "Don't worry—I'm not feeling sorry for you or nothin'. It's me. That peeling part is pretty disturbing."

But she was studying his sketch. "This is too much work."

"It'll take a little time."

"That's true." She looked up at him. The playful smile was gone, and the message was clear. *Do you want me around, or not?* "You said I could help."

"*Real* shoes." The smile was back. "If there's enough lumber, I can do this for little or nothing. You take an inventory of what's in the barn while I finish ripping this up. From what I can tell, the stuff out there is all treated lumber, which this isn't. So I'm thinking…" He slapped the paper with the back of his hand. "This was meant to be."

"Meant to be." She nodded. "I never met the people who lived here, but they left so much of themselves behind, I feel like I know them. They were going to build something out of that pile of lumber. An outdoor something, right?" She laid her hand on the lid of his toolbox. "Can I use your tape measure?"

He lifted one shoulder. "You can just eye-ball it."

"I tend to estimate on the wishful side."

"Oh, yeah." He laughed. "They say that's a woman thing."

"They also say it works to a man's advantage sometimes."

"But not in this case." He handed her the tape measure. "Width, length and thickness. All of it matters."

"Gotcha. I'll write everything down and prepare a report. I have both Excel and PowerPoint."

He winked at her. "So do I." He leaned across the toolbox and gave her a kiss. "Look, Ma. No headache."

The storm rolled in suddenly. Barn swallows went silent, and the air stopped moving in prelude, but Celia kept counting, pulling the tape out, letting it snap back into place and making notes. She was almost finished.

Then daylight dimmed, and the wind took charge of the world. Celia began clutching her notes and searching for the cell phone that only worked half the time, but she froze mid-rush. The skies had opened, and the deluge hammered the barn's ramshackle roof. Celia truly hated being alone in a storm. She considered making a dash for the house, but a flash of lightning turned her away from the door. She wasn't even going to try to roll the mammoth thing shut.

Water had already started to fall through the holes in the roof. There were three steady streams. Fortunately they ended on the floor's two empty stalls and a concrete slab. She'd have to fix those. She was going to use this barn for something. Someday.

She decided to get back to work on her building materials inventory. Better than sitting there listening to heaven clashing with hell.

"Celia!"

Her heartbeat leaped into overdrive as she turned to find Cougar standing—barely—one arm braced on the doorjamb, chest heaving, hat gone, hair dripping.

"You can quit now," he called to her.

And she came running. "My goodness, you're soaked."

He looked at her as though she'd grown a beak. "Do you see what's out there?"

"A storm." She gestured toward the track

door. "I couldn't close it." Not that she'd tried. "This will blow over."

"This place could go with it," he shouted as he grabbed the door and gave it a mighty shove. The noise level dropped by half. "What the hell are you doing? I thought you'd be in the house."

She rammed one hand against her hip. "Do *you* see what's out there?"

"I closed up the camper, turned Flyboy out and then went back to the house thinking that's where you'd be. In the basement, for God's sake."

"I didn't realize..."

He was looking around. "The car." He grabbed her by the arm and pulled her toward the far side of the barn. "Just in case the roof caves in," he said as he set about rolling the canvas from bumper to trunk and over the roof. He jerked the back door open and gave a sweeping gesture. "Party of two?"

She scooted across the cracked leather seat, and he followed her. "Wow, this is some back-seat," she said. "Actual leg room. And it really is pretty clean." She braced her forearm on his shoulder and felt around for the hard lump under her bottom. It was a giant buckle. "Hey, they had seat belts in those days. You're soaked, Cougar. Are you cold?"

"If I say yes, will you tell me to take off my wet clothes?"

He smiled at her when she touched his wet hair. "You lost your hat."

"I tossed it in the back door of the house." He laughed. "Hell, that's the first thing I thought of."

"And the horse was the next, and then the camper."

He shrugged out of his shirt and hung it over the front seat. "How long have you lived here?"

"Almost a year and a half."

"Okay, I should've gone looking for you right after I took care of the hat." He lifted his arm around her shoulders. His chest was brawny, bronze and smooth, and his arms exuded power. "You look up and see those wall clouds forming, you get yourself underground, woman."

"I really don't like the way you say *woman*." She shrugged. "Okay, I didn't look outside."

"Geez."

"I was almost finished with my inventory." She thrust the paper under his nose. "Look."

"I'm wet."

"Well, it's a lot of lumber." She tossed the paper over the front seat. "Did you happen to hear anything on the radio? Anything about where the storm is headed?"

"Mark should be okay," he assured her quietly as he unclipped her hair. "This thing came out of the Hills, tracking east."

Her voice rose when she said, "They went north," then dropped. "But you can't be sure."

"You can never be sure."

"I shouldn't have let him go."

"Yeah, you should've kept him here. He could've been sittin' here in the car with us, wondering whether we're gonna get to see Oz." He ran splayed fingers through her hair. "But he isn't."

She glanced askance. "I wonder if that radio works."

"I wonder if this baby's been sittin' here since 1966. It's in great shape. Somebody sure loved her." He leaned over the seat and turned a couple of knobs, which brought nothing forth. He came back to her laughing. "Can't believe I did that."

"Neither can I, but thanks for trying." She cuddled up to him again. His skin had gone from wet-hot to cool-clammy. "You're cold, aren't you."

"I'm gonna say *yes* and see where it gets me."

She smiled and stroked his shoulder. "I wonder if anybody ever went to a drive-in movie in this car. Or went parking by the river."

"Or got his girl pregnant."

"Or just lost her virginity."

He tucked one hand beneath the hem of her T-shirt, his eyes plying the depths of hers. "Did you?"

"Not in this car. Did you?"

"Not in any car." He ran his fingertips across her abdomen slowly, following her waistband around back. "I've never owned a car. Or gotten a girl pregnant."

"Would you like to?"

His hand stilled, and he gave her an incredulous look.

"Own a car," she said with a smile. "I can tell you like this one."

"Right now, between owning an old car and doing what it takes to get a girl pregnant in the backseat of an old car..." He closed his eyes. "Let me think."

She felt her bra go slack. The wind whistled through the barn walls.

"Better make up your mind. We could end up in Oz, where there's no car and no sex."

"I ain't no tin man, honey."

He shifted her in his arms and planted a warm, wet, breath-stealing kiss on and around and within her mouth as proof. She unbuckled his belt, unzipped his pants and found more evidence. His flesh expanded. There was no rust in his joints and no uncertainty in his brain. He was all human, all man, all there for her and easily made ready. He whisked her T-shirt over her head, taking her bra with it, and coddled her breasts with gentle hands and plucking fingers until she was all about getting him inside her, and he pushed her to the point of telling him so.

He loosened her shorts and slipped his hand between her legs. She pressed his flesh hard and heavy until he took her hand away with a reluctant, "Uh-uh. Just let me."

"Cougar..."

"I have no protection for you." He nibbled her earlobe as he explored her with kind, caring fingers. "If I go in, I'll explode before I can get out."

"Cougar..."

"It doesn't get any better than Cougar."

He slid his finger inside her, and she gasped and gave welcome—moisture drawn out by his wondrous finger to the so, so sensitive flesh between her outer folds. Her whole being followed his woman-centered stroking until it was she who exploded. He held her, pet her, protected her with his sheltering body, giving her the most while she made the best of his gift.

And then she returned his gift in kind. She pressed him back against the car door, lowered his jeans, took him in her mouth and made him let go and let Celia.

They held each other, hands stirring over each other. The car smelled of nothing but their sex, and the storm swirled around them like music, rocking, rolling, finally winding down.

"It's letting up," he said, and she looked up at him, smiling. He smiled back. He rolled his eyes heavenward. "Outside."

Reluctantly they covered themselves, straightened and zipped and buttoned.

"It's gonna be mud city," he said. "What kind of shoes are you wearing?"

"The good kind." She lifted her foot for his inspection. "The washable kind."

"South Dakota gumbo will eat those things up."

"My feet are washable, too. You have some footwear snobbery going on, Cougar."

"I'd pity you if I didn't know you had boots." He sat up. "It's a long way to the house, but, hell, I've done ten times that with at least two-twenty on my back."

"Oh, goodie, a piggyback ride."

"But that was before I took a load of shrap-nel." He glanced down at his knees. "And I've got my boots to consider."

"But you saved your hat."

"Let's just stay here a while." He put his arm around her. "This is my first time."

"Right."

"First time in the backseat of a car. I've always wanted to steam up the windows like this." He drew a heart in the vapor and wrote *CB+*. He glanced at her, the corner of his mouth twitching. And then he drew a *C*. "It fits."

She pulled his head down and kissed him soundly. A second kiss, and a third, and then they looked at each other. *To be continued.*

"My place or yours?" he asked as he opened the car door.

"How big is your shower?"

"About half the size of this backseat, but with a little more head room."

"I'll race you to the house," she proposed

as she emerged from the car. "Bare feet versus boots."

They reached the barn door, he pulled it open, and they surveyed the scene. Cottonwood branches, roof shingles and tumbleweeds littered the yard, but it was the gigantic puddles in what had been dry ground that impressed them the most.

"Yard of a thousand lakes," he said.

"That's what I love about this country," she said. "No half measures."

He sat down on a three-legged stool and pulled one boot off. She laughed. "You can start now if you want," he said without looking up. "I'll still beat the pants off you."

"Not if I get to yours first."

Chapter Eight

Celia took off running, pumping her arms and paddling the air with a flip-flop in each hand. Suddenly reborn, the kid in Cougar sprang from the stool and dashed past her. He carried his boots like a running back, deftly dodging puddles until she started gaining on him by running straight up the middle. He cut in front of her, and she let out a girlish shriek. Music to a bad boy's ears.

He did a one-eighty and sloshed backward. "Take me down, woman. I dare you."

She kicked water in his direction, but he was out of range.

"Aw, c'mon." He fired back, and she was fully splattered. "Try again. The ol' college try. You went to college for this, didn't you?"

A girlish screech added some power to her second try, and he took some spray.

"Better, but not by mu—" One foot went out from under him and down he went, flat on his ass in six inches of water.

Squealing with delight, Celia hurled herself on top of him. Her rubber sandals floated away as she pushed against his shoulders, going for the pin. He couldn't let her get it, but he admired her cowboy try.

"Takedown!" She scooped water on him

furiously with both hands. "Say it! I've got you down!"

"Takedown? Ha! It's first and goal." Tucked under his elevated wing, the ball was still in his possession.

"Typical man." She sat back and scowled. "Not only do you change the rules to suit you, you switch games." Her eyes narrowed. She wagged her finger at his boots and smiled impishly. "But your boots are wet."

He glanced askance. Sure enough. "I don't care about a little water."

"Oh. Now you change your whole bottom line."

"Which is underwater." He grinned, and then he gave her a quick kiss. "As long as my boots aren't caked with mud, I'm happy."

"What about winning the race?"

"What about you beatin' my pants off?"

She hit him with a parting handful of water as she sprang off his lap. Then she reached for his hand. He gave her a wary look, and she laughed. "I'd pity you if you hadn't shown your true colors." She risked a closer reach. "Can we call it a draw?"

"*You* can." He took her hand. "I call it a time-out."

They sloshed through the water, unflinching now that caution and dignity had been released to the wind. He couldn't remember the last time he'd indulged himself in the feel of being ankle-deep in mud, but it felt vaguely familiar. Celia was dragging him toward the grass around the house, but he pulled back at the edge to partake of a thorough mud squeeze between his toes. He looked up and found the teacher smiling, like he'd just mastered some skill. They both laughed. They wiped their feet on wet grass and hosed each other off before they went inside.

He hung back and watched her make the switch from playful girl to real mother. She went directly to the phone, called the school and was, from what he gathered, reassured that the storm hadn't disrupted the field trip.

"Where's your dryer?" he asked as she bustled around in the kitchen—out of sight, back in, out again. He was just standing there, trying to figure out what to do with his hands. "I'll just throw my pants in since you didn't beat them off me." She leaned back around the corner and leered at him. "What?" He yanked at his belt, grinning. Her eyes narrowed. "You've already seen the best parts."

"Oh." The word was injected with a full measure of disappointment. She extended her palm with a supple twist of the wrist. "Hand them over, then."

"Yours are wet, too."

"Yeah, but I've just decided to save mine."

"Fair enough. This way to the shower?" He jerked his thumb over his shoulder. She waved a gimme gesture. "You're not beating anything off me, woman. Turn around."

He took his jeans off, draped them over her arm, and headed for the shower. No rush. He could tell when she turned to take a peek at his bare ass. He had the ears of an owl.

"I'll leave the door unlocked," he said.

He helped himself to soap and shampoo, which was cascading over his face when she slid in behind him, slipped her arms around his waist and pressed her belly against his backside. She slid up a little, down and up again, buffing him with her soft skin and springy hair, her fingertips lightly circling his belly. She stilled momentarily when the tip of his penis touched the back of her hand, but she started in again, pressing a little more, testing him. She'd find him solid if that was what she was testing for. Physically, at least.

He turned in her arms and pivoted with her to give her a turn under the running water. She sputtered, tipped her head and let the water wash her hair as she caressed his backside. "You're a hardass, you know."

"You like that?"

She laughed. "Who knew such a thing existed in real life?"

"You're a soft touch." He slid his hands up

her sleek back, pressed his lip to her forehead. "You know that?"

"I meant literally."

"I meant inside and out." Which both pleased and troubled him, but rubbing up against her in the shower, he wasn't in any mood for trouble. "Let me touch both."

"I want this." She slipped her hand between their bodies and claimed his penis. "This was made to touch me inside."

"You sure? I had the feeling you weren't impressed."

"I didn't say it was made to look at." She hooked her leg around his back and lifted herself as though she would shimmy up his body. "I said... I meant..."

He put one arm around her and used the other to ease himself down in the tub with her in his lap, right where she'd been when they'd played in the mud puddle like kids. "I'm made to go deep," he warned.

She rose on her knees and positioned herself to take him where he was made to fit her, to swallow him by degrees, feel him make his way in a place built to house him and home in on him and welcome him with her undying "Yesss..." until the whole of him made her catch her breath.

He went still. "Hurt?"

"No. Yes."

But she was in charge. She looked into his eyes as though he were a mirror and she was learning a new dance, taking it slow, trying one rhythm, then another, all the while watching his eyes. He had no idea what she saw, but he saw pleasure. Behind those beautiful brown eyes there was pleasure and nothing else. There was Cougar and no one else. He would be good to her, and she would make him even better.

He took charge. He found ways to reach her that made her body quake and her mouth pour molten words in his ears. Ah, she was flying, and he wanted to stay where he was and fly with her, first class.

But he did not.

"No!" she gasped, but she could do nothing to keep him from pulling himself away. In his arms she was boneless and mindless and beautifully spent, oblivious to the water pelting her back.

"Oh, I could have gone on all day," she whispered against his shoulder.

"That's where we're different. Where we

have to part ways if I'm unprepared." He kissed her wet hair. "I'll do better next time."

Her throaty chuckle felt like a bee buzzing against his chest. "It doesn't get any better than Cougar."

"Oh, yeah. Cougar gets better than Cougar." He lifted her shoulders away from his. "What? You're laughing at my name?" She braced her hands on his arms and glanced down between them. "No, don't look down. If you look down and you're still laughing, I'll be—"

She kissed him hard and quick. "I'm laughing for joy, silly."

"That's something I've never been called. Silly." He raised a palm against the spray. "Get up, woman. It was nice while it lasted, but the water's going cold on us."

They laughed at themselves in their awkward recovery. He reached past her and shut the water off. "Joy, huh?" He grinned. "That good?"

"You're that good, Cougar." She slid the shower curtain aside, grabbed a bath sheet from the rack and flung it around his shoulders. "Not it, Cougar. You."

"Joy seems way out there. Just tell me the sex was good. I get that." He took a couple of swipes at his legs with the towel, and then he wrapped it around her. "It's been a while, Celia. I kept it together tour after tour, and then I got hit, and I lost it. I can't even tell you what I lost and how much I got back. You're taking a risk with me."

"It's always a risk."

She climbed out of the tub, and he stood

there, watching her dry off. She stepped into a pair of silky-looking white panties and slipped lacy bra straps over her shoulders. He stepped out of the tub, took the two sides of the bra band from her hands and fit the tiny wire hooks together. Pleased with the steadiness, he kissed her shoulder.

"Are you trying to scare me?"

"That's the last thing I wanna do. Scare you, hurt you. If it happens, tell me. Okay? And I'll go."

She turned to him. "I want you here, and so does Mark."

"For now." He glanced at the door. "When does Mark get back?"

"Soon. I'll go get your jeans out of the dryer." She pulled a fresh, pale green T-shirt on over wet hair and climbed into a pair of clean shorts. "We could use some wind now to dry everything out." She twisted her hair up the back of her head and clipped it in place.

He listened to the sound of bare feet go down the hall, then up again. The door opened, and his pants came in on the end of her arm.

"Here you go. I need to be at the highway to meet the bus pretty soon. I just hope my road's passable."

"We'll take the pickup," Cougar called out after her, chuckling at the way she bounced between shy and seductive.

And then Celia gasped. He knew distress when he heard it. Before she'd finished demanding, "What are you doing here?" Cougar was at her side.

"He's quick," Greg said. He was seated

comfortably in an easy chair in the least conspicuous corner of the living room. "Quick as a cat. What do you do for a living, Cougar?"

A pale red haze closed in from the periphery like rising smoke. Cougar stared through it, focusing impassively at the intruder. Inches away, Celia's body exuded tension.

But she spoke quietly. "What are you doing in my house?"

"I heard about the storm. It kinda blew through ahead of me." Banyon cut his eyes at Cougar. "Looks like that's not all."

Cougar's blood was heating up.

"Get out of here," Celia demanded, her tone on the rise. "This is *my house*. You can't just walk in here."

"Anybody could. The front door was unlocked. And the road *is* passable." Banyon pushed himself out of the chair and closed in. "Where's my son?"

"Mark is in school."

"How do you know? For all you know, the school could've blown away." He turned to Cougar. "I guess you noticed, Cecilia's a great lay during a—"

Cougar had the intruder in a headlock with his arm behind his back before the sentence could be finished with anything more than a choking sound. "Yeah, I'm quick. And you're trespassing."

"Cougar..."

"What do you want me to do with him, Celia?"

"I just want him to go away." He couldn't look at her, but her hand felt cool on his arm. "Don't, Cougar. Please."

"You can't just walk into somebody's house," Cougar calmly told his prisoner. "It's against the law."

"Cougar, let him go. He'll leave." The hand on his arm tightened. "Please, Cougar."

He released the head of the prisoner first and then the arm.

"I think you broke my arm," Banyon whined, cradling one arm in the other.

"I know something about breaking bones. I thought about it, but I decided against it." Cougar stepped back. "The smart thing for you to do now is leave."

"This man's dangerous." Banyon stepped to one side, effectively using Celia as a shield. "Why is he here?"

"Because I invited him, Greg. And he—"

"And he was here first? But he isn't the

first, is he?" Another sidestep, menacing eyes, loading up the idiot finger and aiming at Cougar...

Buster, you're about to blunder.

"You aren't the first. I was the first, but between me and you there was a whole damn parade. A whole—"

Cougar backhanded the fool's mouth shut, spun him around and neutralized his "broken" arm.

"Aaa! I'm...calling...the police."

"You." Pressure applied. "Are." More pressure applied. "Trespassing." And Banyon was out the door.

Cougar closed the door and stood for a moment, cooling himself, calming himself, collecting himself. He turned to face Celia, whose eyes were big with surprise but not—so far—horror.

"He'll call the police," she said in a small voice.

Meaning what? "Did I do something wrong?"

"I would have called the police." She took a tentative step. "If he'd tried to hurt anyone, I *would* have."

"What do you think he was he trying to do?"

"I don't care what he says, and it doesn't matter anymore what he suspects. He's a bully and a coward."

"One thing I'm not is a coward."

"You're not a bully, either." She wrapped her arms around her slender middle. "When Greg comes here, I don't ask him to come in. He had no business..." Her face went funny with a touch of sadness, a hint of fury. "He doesn't come in my house, but he comes to take my son." She shook her head. "*Our* son according to the court."

He wanted to hold her, but he wasn't sure what category he fell into. Maybe she wasn't looking at a bully, but what business did he have?

"He won't get past me, Celia."

"He'll make trouble for you." She closed the distance between them. "He has a way of twisting things. Finding you here…"

"Are we doing something wrong?"

"No, of course not." She put her arms around him. "Mark and I are both glad you're here. But I don't want you to get mixed up with Greg."

"Too late." He rubbed her back. "He's the one who got mixed up with me."

"And I'm so sorry for that. If I hadn't brought you your jeans…"

"I *really* would've scared the crap out of him." He leaned back and smiled at her. "Let's go down to the bus stop and wait for Mark."

The bus was late, but the word from the school was reassuring. The group had been treated to ice cream and playtime while they waited out the storm. Like hood ornaments on his pickup, Celia and Cougar sat high above the river in the right of way on the muddy island that her turnoff had become. They didn't speak of the day's roller coaster ride. For her part, Celia put doubts aside and took pleasure in the lingering afterglow of love made with exquisite care. Blowing fresh off rain-washed prairie grass, the cool breeze toyed with her hair and soothed her head. The growing connection between her heart and that of the man at her side could only be a good thing.

At first glimpse of bright yellow, Cougar jumped down and turned to offer her a hand. "Mark won't be hungry right away, will he? We should check on Flyboy. How's your fence out there?"

"I haven't checked."

"Well, you've had no reason to. If the horse is gone, we'll put out an APB."

"Really? Can you do that?"

He smiled. "We'll find him. There's no driving out there now, but I think I can borrow a horse from Logan."

She loved that warm, reassuring smile of

his. He had one for Mark when he got off the bus, and Mark gave him one right back. Celia didn't mind seeing Mark reach for Cougar's hand without a thought for where hers might be.

Vicky Long Soldier leaned around the safety pole and reported, "We had a good day."

"Heard the Thunder Bird flew south of you," Cougar said. "You missed a hell of a show."

"You guys get any damage?"

"Nothing a good hired man can't fix."

Celia gave him a look as the bus pulled away. "Hired man?"

"Yes, ma'am." Cougar adjusted his hat as he glanced at the bulbous layers of white clouds pressing against the horizon. "I thought *remodeling contractor* might be pushin' it."

Celia loved the way he made her laugh. She grabbed his face and pulled his head within reach of her quick, firm kiss. The surprised look on his face delighted her even more. She looked down at her son and saw the innocent marriage of Cougar's surprise and her own delight. Life was good again.

Cougar's four-wheel drive attacked mud like an army half track. As they approached the fence, he signaled Mark in the backseat, pointed to the windshield, and then turned his hand into an airplane. The spotted mustang stood half a mile away.

Cougar got out of the pickup and loaded Mark onto his back, but once they reached the fence, the boy had other plans. He got down and started trying to pull up grass. Cougar waved off Celia's pending objection, took out a pocket knife and squatted beside Mark to lend a hand. Wheatgrass and big bluestem with edible leaves and nodding heads—the boy knew what he wanted. He took the handful Cougar cut for him, walked to the fence and waved it like a semaphore. Ears forward, the horse trotted in their direction.

"Wow," Celia whispered. "Oh, wow."

Mark kept waving, and the horse kept coming. He stopped a few yards short of the fence. Mark got down on hands and knees and started ripping the grass again. Flyboy lowered his nose to the ground and took several steps closer.

"I'll be damned. If it wasn't for the fence…"

Mark looked up at Cougar. Celia held her

breath. The light in her son's living eye spoke volumes. *If it wasn't for the fence.*

Cougar stepped the bottom strand down and pulled the middle one up enough to allow Mark to slip through. He stood quietly, clutching his handful of grass. Flyboy hung his head and slowly closed the distance. He snuffled the boy's shoulder, nickered and sniffed the grass.

And Mark nickered back.

Mark made a sound.

Celia's mouth dropped open. She wanted to whinny or howl or crow. She wanted to squeal and squeeze and jiggety jig. She'd wanted and waited and wished, and she was about to explode.

Cougar took hold of her hand. She looked up at him, and he shook his head almost imperceptibly, as though the slightest motion might destroy the magic. They watched the two sensitive creatures bring all their senses to bear for an E.T. moment. Mark stood quietly while Flyboy ate the grass from his hand.

A car drove up behind them and killed the moment. Cougar ignored it, but Celia looked over her shoulder. It was brown and white with a lightbar on the roof. Her heart sank. She heard the horse retreat and felt the loss of Cougar's hand. He was stretching wire again, making a hole for Mark to climb through. Celia reached for him as soon as he crossed over. Whatever was going on, her child would not be touched by it.

The county sheriff was an older man, slightly paunchy, but he carried himself smartly, sported a tan Stetson and wore a star affixed to his neatly pressed khaki shirt. Celia had heard him speak at a teacher's meeting, where he and the chief of tribal police had explained the nature of their separate but cooperative jurisdictions in Indian country.

"Is your name Cougar?" he asked without preamble.

"That's right."

"First, last?"

"Both."

The sheriff put hands to hips. "We got a call about an assault. Are you a tribal member?"

"Not here. I'm from Wind River."

"Mrs. Banyon?" Celia nodded, and the sheriff touched his hat brim. "Sheriff Pete Harding. Can you tell me what happened here today?"

"Why don't we let Mrs. Banyon take the

boy inside, and you have your talk with me, Sheriff?"

Sheriff Harding looked down at Mark and appeared to consider the suggestion. "Was the boy here when the incident happened?"

"Mark just got home from summer school," Celia said. "Would you like to come inside?"

Celia was unsure of the protocol for an official visit from the sheriff. Should she ask to see a warrant or refuse to say anything without benefit of counsel? So far, Cougar hadn't batted an eye. But, then he'd been icily calm earlier, too, and the only thing he'd batted was Greg. Who'd deserved it.

She set Mark in front of the TV with a video game and joined Cougar and the sheriff at the kitchen table. The sheriff had opened up a metal clipboard and was filling out a form.

"My ex-husband came into my house un-invited," Celia blurted out. Cougar looked at her, his expression unreadable. Had she spoken too soon?

"Broke in?"

"Walked in." Celia folded her hands on the table. "The door wasn't locked. He scared me, insulted me. The very fact that he walked in was a threat."

The sheriff flipped a page in his clipboard. "He said he was looking for his son."

"Today wasn't his day."

"I guess not," the sheriff said without looking up from his previous notes. "He thought his arm was broken."

"It wasn't," Cougar said. "Did he file a complaint on me?"

"He complained, yeah." Harding turned

to Celia. "Do you have a restraining order against Mr. Banyon?"

"Not yet."

"If he's threatening you, you should get one." Back to Cougar. "He says you tried to strangle him."

Cougar gave a humorless chortle.

"Said you knew karate or something." Harding scanned his report and appeared to read from it. "He's pretty sure your hands could be considered dangerous weapons."

"Are you gonna arrest me?"

"I don't know." The sheriff gave himself away with a hint of a smile. "Are your hands dangerous weapons?" No answer. "Army or Marines?"

"Army."

"Were you in the Middle East?" Cougar

nodded. The sheriff turned to Celia. "Is Mr. Cougar living here with you?"

"Talk to me, Sheriff. I'm Cougar. I'll answer your questions."

"Are you living with—"

"He's working for me," Celia said.

"Okay, so who's answering my questions?"

"I live in that camper out back." Cougar leaned in. "You need probable cause to arrest me, so let's get to the story, Sheriff. Yes, I know how to handle an intruder without breaking any bones or scarring him for life."

"I was in the Marines," Harding said.

"That's not my problem."

The sheriff stared for a moment. Finally he chuckled. Nothing uproarious, but a bit of an icebreaker.

Celia sighed. *Let's get this over with.*

"I came into the living room, found Greg sitting there—scared me half to death—and I asked him to leave. He said some things, and Cougar took exception."

"Mr. Banyon took exception to Mr. Cougar's exception," the sheriff concluded. "Turned out Banyon had no injuries. I took his statement at the clinic."

"So you're not going to arrest anyone," Cougar said.

"Do you want to make a complaint, Mrs. Banyon?" Sheriff Harding pulled another form from his clipboard. "I can take yours now and file them both."

"About Greg just walking in here?"

"It's up to you. If you decide to ask for a restraining order, a record of this incident would be…" He gave her a pointed look. "It's up to you."

She took his point. Clearly Greg had acted like a jackass when he'd reported his outrage to the sheriff. Celia knew Greg's routine better than anyone. She'd hoped to put it behind her. She'd pulled up stakes and *moved,* for pity's sake.

"Yes, I want to make a complaint," she said with a sigh. "I want the whole incident on record."

The sheriff slid the form across the table and laid his pen down on top of it. Celia picked it up and set about telling her side of the story. She kept it brief and purely factual, squeezing her emotions between the lines, where no one would see them. But she knew they were there. She owned them. And she was unapologetic about filing the report, the kind she'd never wanted to make because things just weren't that bad.

But neither was filing the complaint.

"There's no room at the County Inn right now," Harding said as he slipped the new reports into his handy metal case. "You're right. If you did what Banyon accused you of, you did it well. Not a mark on him. Since he's the one trespassing, I have no cause to arrest anyone here." He turned to Celia as he snapped his clipboard shut. "The number is 911."

"I didn't handle that very well," Celia said quietly. They sat together on the sofa. Several feet away, Mark was busy communicating with jumpy Lego figures through a joystick. "I should have called right away, the minute I walked out and found him here. I was afraid of…"

"Of what? Him? Me?" He turned on her as the truth hit him. "*For* me? Don't worry about me, Celia. You do what's right for you and Mark."

"I was taken off guard. Blindsided, really."

"Celia…"

"It's been quite a day." She laid her hand on his thigh.

He covered it quickly with his as though he took exception. She almost said, *I'm not going to do anything,* but she started to pull her hand away instead.

He held fast. "If he showed up that way again, I can't promise I'd do anything different."

"We'll call the sheriff."

"*You'll* call the sheriff. You'll do what you need to do. As for me…" He gave a wistful smile. "Greg was lucky."

"He's all talk. Don't let him get to you. He's one of those people who would sue you because he broke into your house and got bitten by your dog." She squeezed his hand. "No more fighting."

"That wasn't a fight. All I did was shut him up and move him out."

"I'm glad Mark wasn't here." She leaned closer. "You heard him, right? His voice?" Cougar smiled. "That was his voice. It's been so long since I've heard it, Cougar, but I knew it would come back. *He* would come back."

"Let him do it in his own way, his own time."

"You said horses were part of your therapy. Did you…?" *His own way.* "I mean, were you…?" *His own time.*

"I've been around horses most of my life. Thought I knew all about them. I could use them. I could get them to do what I wanted them to do. And I knew they were smart, too. People think the smartest animals are the ones you can train to be most like humans."

"The ones who let you put diapers on them and teach them to smoke?"

He laughed. "Can you see a horse putting up with that? No." He shook his head. "When I was in the hospital—and I was there for months—they said I needed to do something besides read and go to the gym. I needed to connect. So I looked at what they had to offer, and there was this horse therapy. I laughed. Horse *therapy?* Okay, I could connect. I knew horses." He smiled. "But I never realized how much they knew about me."

She glanced at Mark. "Can you explain it to me?"

"You read the book, honey." He grinned. "You're right about Logan. He's the master. He's the one to explain it all." He jammed his thumb to his chest. "I know it in here. I know where Mark's been, and I think I know where he is now. You're right, Celia. He's coming back."

She closed her eyes and drew a deep breath. "I'm so glad he wasn't here today."

"Yeah. I am, too."

Celia would never know how glad he was. Cougar's heart ached with it. He knew it wouldn't have made a difference who'd been there to witness his battle with himself.

Banyon was no match for him. He wasn't dealing with a trained watchdog. Celia had a wildcat patrolling the premises. A good hard-ass could run interference for her, but she needed more than that. She needed a man, and she deserved a whole one. Cougar was on his way back, too, just like Mark was.

But would he ever get there?

"And it *has* been a hell of a day." He slapped his knees. "We're going out for supper."

Chapter Nine

"Truce, Cecilia."

The bread truck door sounded like a lid slamming shut on a tin box. Celia had seen it coming, but she'd kept right on currying the big gray saddle horse, so much more deserving of her attention than the driver of that damn truck. Grooming a horse on the shady side of the barn was her favorite chore at the Double D. It was therapeutic.

Dealing with Greg would require all the tranquility she'd attained.

"See?" He took off his cap and waved it above his head. "White flag. We have business to discuss."

"I don't want you coming here, Greg." She turned to the tool bucket and traded the currycomb for a body brush. "I work here."

"You volunteer here. It isn't like you're punching a time clock." He pulled up short as soon as he hit the shade. "If you're reasonable about this, it'll only take a minute, and look—" He made a sweeping gesture, taking in the view of three teenagers stacking square bales with Hoolie Hoolihan, who'd been ranch foreman since Sally and Ann were children. "Witnesses."

Hoolie noticed Greg's gesture and started

moving in their direction. Any other time Celia would have welcomed the older man's conversation, but she didn't want anything to prolong Greg's stay. "No, we're okay, Hoolie," she called out as she waved him back.

"Just here to say hi," Greg added.

"And what else?" Celia asked quietly.

He jammed his hat back on. "Hey, I went by your place, didn't go inside, didn't even get out of the van. Your car wasn't there, but his pickup was. Sounds like you've got him doing a little carpentry out there." He glanced over his shoulder. "Anyway, I saw your car here."

She was going to start parking behind the barn. She stared at the big sliding door. Maybe she could fit her little car in one of the stalls. Her question was still hanging in Greg's aggravating limbo.

"Where's Mark? Did you leave him with that Indian?"

"Mark has school this week. You have his schedule. What business do we have to discuss?"

"We got a settlement offer."

Celia turned to apply the big brush to Tank's gray coat, running her free hand over the warm hair.

"Tichner says it's good, but they'll do a lot better. Insurance companies don't want to go to court on a case like this. Loss of an eye is bad enough, but there's obviously serious brain damage. Speech, hearing—no matter what the doctors say, none of that's functioning. I mean, it's been how long now?"

She turned and stared at him, knowing her eyes looked as cold as he made her feel.

"Almost three years, right? So Tichner says we turn the offer down. Look at this. He says we can do way better. We have to, right? I mean, the lawyers take a third after they pay every cost they can come up with. So we both need to sign off on this."

"I'm not signing anything."

"Why not?"

"I'll get in touch with the lawyer myself." She kept on talking while she put the brush back in the rubber bucket and gave Hoolie a high sign, pointing to the horse. Hoolie signaled back. "We're going to go back to communicating through third parties. I feel like you're stalking me."

"So you got yourself a bodyguard?"

"I'm going inside," she told him. "I'm not signing anything except a restraining order if you don't stop this. And I don't care how many lawyers you hire."

"You're lucky I didn't press charges on your boyfriend."

She kept walking.

"My lawyer has a private investigator—"

Damn. He was following her. She didn't want a scene. Not here. This was *the sanctuary.*

"Leave me alone, Greg."

Sally's husband, Hank, appeared on the porch. "What's up, Celia? Is this guy lost?"

"I wish he'd *get* lost," she grumbled as she mounted the steps to the big covered porch. Greg cursed under his breath and began to head back toward his truck.

"I'll be glad to give him the message."

"No, Hank, it's okay. The sheriff's already

taken dueling complaints over Greg's little tussle with Cougar."

"That must've been fun to watch. You didn't get a video, did you?"

"It's not something I want to see again. Once was…" She smiled at the tall, rangy Indian cowboy with the stony face and kind eyes. "Actually, once was pretty thrilling, but don't tell anyone. Is Sally…"

"She's taking a little siesta." He glanced past her. "The bread man is leaving."

The truck door slammed, the engine roared and the tires squealed.

Celia closed her eyes and sighed. "I'm sorry, Hank."

"For what? He's your ex for a reason. If he chooses to go around with the reason as good as tattooed across his forehead, that's not your fault." She opened her eyes and was greeted with a smile. "Just makes us love you all the more."

"It's Mark I'm worried about. That man's his father."

"We love Mark, too. Sally has a special affinity for him."

"That's why I wanted to talk to her. Mark has made real progress since we've been coming here, and now with Cougar's horse…" She was almost afraid to tell anyone. She might jinx it. "Something really amazing is happening."

"You want to have a seat and tell me about it?" Hank gave a nod in the direction of a pair of high-backed porch rockers. "I know a little something about therapy. And rodeo cowboys get their share of head injuries."

Celia dropped into the chair and rocked back, taking comfort in the soothing motion. Hank was a physician's assistant who worked the rodeo circuit with a sports medicine team. He was also a farrier. He understood the nature of healing and what it took to promote the process.

"The mustang—they named him Flyboy— twice now Flyboy has walked right up to Mark and put his head down so they could check each other out."

The other rocker squeaked as Hank took a seat. He gave her his full attention, eyes lowered respectfully in the Indian way. "They haven't done that much with him," Celia explained. "No hackamore or halter, no saddle blanket, nothing like that. Cougar just finished repairing the corral."

"At your place?"

"That's another thing I wanted to tell Sally. She can add that to Cougar's paperwork. The horse is at my place now."

She didn't know why she felt compelled to explain the horse's whereabouts in the middle of her miracle story. Maybe her news didn't surprise him that much. Or maybe he was respectfully multi-tasking.

Keep it light, Celia. The neighbors don't need any more complications.

"I'd love to have her come out and inspect it."

"Oh, I'm sure she'll wanna look into this situation. You and Cougar?" Hank chuckled. "She'll be on the phone with Mary Wolf Track as soon as she gets an update. Those women had you pegged for a couple the night of Mary's medal celebration."

"Sally must not have enough to do."

"Right." Hank rocked back. "I'd like to see Mark with his Flyboy myself. Seems like it might be a little risky, putting them together this soon."

"Mark marches to the beat of his own drum. He got in there with the horse when we were standing close by. Cougar was right behind him, but then it just happened. It was like they made a connection. Mark and Flyboy."

"I believe it. Horses are wondrous creatures. I never realized how amazing they are until I fell in with these mustangs." He flashed her a bright-eyed smile. "And Mustang Sally."

"I was thinking…I know you've got a lot

going on here, but what about a horse therapy program?"

"For who?"

"Cougar…" She was going too far too fast. She lifted one shoulder. "Well, Cougar's had some experience with a…special program."

"For kids?"

Celia shook her head tightly.

"For veterans." He needed no confirmation. "So what are you thinking?"

"Right now I'm thinking, *hoping* my son's about to give me ideas. Give *us* ideas. He's on the verge of a breakthrough, Hank. He's been to so many doctors, and not one of them has been able to reach him the way these horses have."

"We've got our hands full here. 'Course you start talking to Sally, she'll grow another hand." He patted hers. "Or match up a new pair."

"It's just the germ of an idea."

"Don't tell her that. Sally loves germs." He gave a chin jerk in the direction of the window on the far side of the front door. "She's got files full of them in there. It's a wonder her computer hasn't been quarantined."

"Hey, Night Horse, are you out there rockin' and rollin' with another woman?"

Celia and Hank exchanged mock-guilty glances. He turned his head toward the window again. "She came to see you, but when she found out I was available…"

"Hey, Celia." The front door opened, and Sally stepped onto the porch. She was limping, but she wasn't using her cane. "I didn't know you were on the schedule today."

"I had—" Celia and Hank took to their feet simultaneously "—some extra time."

"Not by my calculations. I had you keeping time with one of our most promising contenders." Sally tucked herself under her new husband's arm. "And not this guy. He doesn't compete." She looked up at Hank. "Or is that compute?" Back to Celia with a sassy smile. "Put it this way, he has no idea what's in my files." She poked her husband three times just above his belt buckle, once for each word. "Must love germs."

Hank laughed. "I thought you were asleep."

"I was, but I put the squeak in these chairs so I don't miss anything." She turned to Celia. "I like your idea. What's Cougar planning to do with that flashy horse he picked? Endurance?"

"I haven't mentioned this therapy thing to him. It's something that just started…incubating. As I was telling Hank, Cougar hasn't gotten that far yet, but I think he has his heart set on endurance. He's done it before."

"That man's made to endure, no question. As far as the heart's concerned, though, these horses have a way of changing hearts. Human hearts. Horse hearts are pretty steady, but human hearts…" She patted Hank's chest. "People think they're headed in one direction, they meet up with wild horses and they get turned around. Find themselves coming full circle."

"Maybe they just find themselves," Hank said. He was clearly the no-nonsense side of the Night Horse equation.

"I like your idea." A slow-rising Sally smile

boded well for *some*body's idea. "Could we make a little video? Mark and Flyboy?"

But maybe not Celia's.

"I don't know about..." Celia glanced at Hank. He rolled his eyes. "What kind of a video?"

"Just a little home movie. Of course, it couldn't be used for anything without your permission, and maybe it wouldn't even turn out to be useful for anything except my extensive files. But it sounds like you've got something going that could help people."

"And horses," Hank said. "The more we discover about them, the better people like having the wild ones around."

"And we need to see the work in progress with Mark," Sally said.

"He's not a guinea pig."

"He's a kid who's building confidence his own way. You try to minimize the risk the best you can, but let him take the next step. These are the good times." Sally spoke from experience. "I like your idea. It's exciting, Celia." She looked up at her husband. "Isn't that right, cowboy? It would be a challenge, but how exciting!"

"What, were you experiencing a dull moment?" Hank raised an eyebrow. "Thanks for spreading your germs around, Celia. Seems my wife had an empty petri dish hidden somewhere."

"I keep them in files, not dishes." Sally laughed. "Ah, cowboys. They love their poetry, but they're forever mixing their metaphors."

"I'll do some research," Celia said.

"Even more excitement," Sally enthused. "Life gives you a little mold, you make penicillin. Without the germs and the people who spread them around, life would be nothing but a bowl of boring cherries."

Now who was mixing metaphors?

Cougar heard the car coming. Celia had gone off to do her thing at the Double D, and she was bringing Mark back with her from the bus stop.

Damn, he needed one more hour to finish up his first satellite deck. But it was usable for tonight. Mark could roast marshmallows in the new fire pit while the Western sky put on its nightly show. Cougar stashed his toolbox out of sight and hurried to meet them as they got out of the car in front of the house.

"Come this way. Eyes closed. Here." He tucked a hand from each of them into the back pockets of his jeans. "Close your eyes and come along like good little tail feathers." He smiled when he reached back to lay his hand over Mark's eyes and found them already closed. The ears were working now.

"Ta-*tum* ta-*tum,*" Cougar chanted, bending knees on the downbeat as he led the dance. Celia had pinned the word *silly* on him, and it seemed to be sticking. "Ho!" The big tail feather crashed into him. The small one did not.

He reached back, pulled precious hands from his pockets and squeezed them as though they were On buttons.

"Ta-da."

Cougar, you are one lovesick puppy.

"Oh, yes." Wide-eyed and thoroughly charmed, Celia stepped up on the wooden hexagon.

He'd cut a square hole for the fire pit in the center—the most time-consuming part of the project—and lined it with fire bricks, which he'd bought without telling her. He'd showed her his plans, but he had the feeling she hadn't expected him to come through. Once he got going on a project, he tended to improvise. He'd added the fire pit during the improvising stage. *Pure genius.*

"Oh, Cougar, this is wonderful."

Music to his ears.

"There'll be a full bench around the edge." He drew a picture in the air. "For tonight we'll use chairs. I picked some sage and got some marshmallows." He caught her looking at him as though he'd really done something, and a wave of diffidence washed over him. "Marsh-mallows first, then sage. You don't want to mix the two."

Fortunately, he wasn't capable of blushing.

"This is beautiful, Cougar." She took a quarter turn around the structure, touched one of the posts that would become part of his benches, and sought his gaze across the corner of his creation. "I hope this isn't tak-ing you away from Flyboy too much. I mean, this is amazing, but I thought the time in the competition was getting short."

"Well, it is. I worked him some this morn-ing." He signaled the boy, who had checked out the fire pit, probably noticed the sand at the bottom and wondered how he was supposed to play in that little thing. "Mark and I are gonna get back to it right now if you wouldn't mind throwing some chow together."

Celia smiled. "No ifs, ands or buts about letting me cook for you?"

"None."

"I love it, Cougar. I love…"

He hung on the word. *Tell me, Celia. I know it's too soon, but say it anyway.*

"…everything you've done here," she said, disappointing him a little, but she walked back to him and hung her arms around his neck.

And his heart soared. "Everything?"

"Every blessed thing."

"Show me." His lips twitched. "Plant one on me, woman."

Her kiss was slow, soft and sweet. There

was sure as hell more to it than a simple *Good job, Cougar.*

She leaned back and smiled, all dreamy-eyed. "I'd cook you a royal feast if I knew what went into one."

"Home-cooked meat and potatoes." He kissed her back, but he wasn't matching her on the slow, soft and sweet. Quick and hard said it better. He stepped back and tucked a wisp of hair behind her ear. "It doesn't get any better than meat and potatoes."

"Home-cooked." She laid her hand on his cheek. "Thank you. I don't know what else to say."

"You'll think of something. You're good with words." He signaled Mark. "C'mon, partner. Let's go fly our pony, boy."

* * *

It was a quiet supper. Cougar had given his big gesture some more thought, and he was feeling a little silly. There it was again. He didn't much like the word, but he liked the feeling even less. He'd gone overboard. He probably looked like one of those cartoon characters with the googlie eyes and throbbing lump in his chest. He could only wish he was a tin man right about now.

Especially since something was bothering Celia, and her skill with words wasn't serving her. Which would have been strictly her business if Cougar hadn't been pretty damn sure her business had a lot to do with him. Not that he was so damned important—she had a kid, for God's sake—but he was a lost soul trying to find himself in her backyard.

Pretty bad for a man to give the woman he loved that kind of business.

She asked him about his horse therapy with the VA, and he probably wasn't any more forthcoming than she was, but he wasn't eager to talk about his time in the hospital. He was trying to move on. Plus, he was pretty sure Mark was really listening, and he didn't want the boy to start thinking of Flyboy as some kind of tool or Cougar as another so-called specialist with a theory. They were just three slightly dislocated males who spoke the same language.

"So all we'll need is a few sticks," he ended up telling her when neither of them could come up with anything the other was looking to hear. "Soak 'em good so they don't burn. There's one puddle left out there we can use."

"I'll do the dishes while you—"

"I'll help you first," he said. "We've got plenty of time."

They cleared the table and did the dishes— she washed and he dried—while Mark played outside. The sun had set, and magic light held its fleeting sway—bright enough to see by, soft enough to smudge all the sharp edges.

Celia leaned closer to the window. "What's he doing?"

"Cutting sticks."

"With what?" She turned to him, horrified. "You gave him a knife?"

"I let him use my pocket knife to cut some twine off a square bale. Forgot to get it back."

"Cougar!"

"You see him, Celia. I showed him how to use the knife. You see this?" He showed her the tiny cut on the pad of his thumb. "I gave some skin to show him what happens." He turned his hand to take a look for himself, just to make sure the evidence was still there. A traditional Indian sacrifice—a bit of skin, a drop of blood. It made sense. Give a little, maybe you won't be shedding a lot.

He nodded toward the window. "There's still plenty of light out. He can see what he's doing. He *knows* what he's doing. Certain things a kid has to learn living out in the country like this."

"Did you show him where to find sticks and what to…"

He shook his head as he dried the last of the plates. "No more than what you heard me say at the table."

"What we both heard." Tears welled in her eyes. "It's true, isn't it?"

"Oh, yeah." He draped the towel over her hands and gently blotted them dry. "It's true."

One of her little wells ranneth over. He caught the runoff with his wounded thumb, and then touched his tongue to it, thirsty for her joy.

"He has to spend this weekend with Greg," she whispered.

He went still. "You haven't seen any sign of any kind of physical…"

She shook her head. "Except that he wants to stay with me. With *us*. He trusts you, Cougar. Maybe more than he does me right now. I'm the one who hands him over to his father."

"You want me to do that for you?"

"No. That's my responsibility. I signed the

damned agreement." She drew his hand to her cheek and kissed his callused palm. "And you couldn't do it anyway. I know you better than you think I do."

"I'd rather eat nails, but I could do that, too, if I had to." He glanced out the window. The first evening star pierced twilight. Mark was arranging his sticks on the new deck. "Maybe I should take a cue from your ex-husband and do some stalking. Nobody stalks better than a Cougar."

"You're a man of many talents," she told him as she pulled a package of marshmallows from the cupboard.

"Master of none." He folded the dishtowel and laid it next to the sink. "Which doesn't matter. Let somebody else write the books. I ain't gonna run for office."

* * *

The embers still glowed in the firepit. Curls of blue-gray smoke filled the air with the scent of wild sage. Mark slept in Cougar's arms. He hardly stirred when Cougar plucked a puff of sticky white stuff from the boy's upper lip, thinking someday he'll grow hair here. He'll kiss a girl. He'll say silly things. He'll laugh when she says silly things back to him. He'll kid her about having his eye on her, and she'll let him kiss her again.

Cougar licked the marshmallow off his finger. His satellite deck had been christened with fire. He'd pointed out ancient star-to-star sketches in the inky sky and told Indian legends about the way they'd formed. He knew different ones—Shoshoni, Lakota, Navaho—

even a few Pashtun tales. He especially liked the one about shooting stars chasing devils.

One of his fellow warriors in Afghanistan—Ahmer, who was a translator and whose name meant *red*—had explained his traditional code of honor, which had a lot in common with some of the values Cougar's own grandfathers had taught him—hospitality, loyalty, community support, the role of shame, ways to settle scores. "Oh, so you would do it this way," one would say, and the other would listen, take exception where there was misunderstanding, and then maybe tell his side.

Ahmer had liked it all over when Cougar told him that red represented goodness and warmth and pleasure in his mother's Lakota tradition. It was the color of the sky at sunrise, and the red road was a good path. Ahmer said, yes, he was a red road kind of a guy. After all, the sun rose in the east. Ahmer's squad would be headed west tomorrow, he'd said. He would consider turning his face to the sun and marching backward, but since guys like Cougar came from the west, such a move would not be prudent.

The next day had been Ahmer's final tomorrow. The direction of the setting sun, where the symbolic color was black, had taken him to his death. Every time Cougar thought of the previous night's conversation, he saw red. He saw the red sky of the rising sun, and he felt its warmth. And then he saw a red explosion.

Go get 'em, shooting stars, he'd cheered as he'd folded his hand around Mark's and combined their power in a skyward fist pump.

Chase those devils to the far corners of the universe. For Ahmer, he'd added silently. For Ahmer's sons. For mine.

And Mark had made a joyful noise. It was small, and it came from deep in his throat, but it was joyful.

Chapter Ten

Before Greg arrived, Cougar and Celia had a quiet discussion safely out of Mark's range. Was it time to take a stand? And if it was, would she give him the place of honor—the badass post between good and ugly? The little smile she gave him was appreciative, but it said *stand down*.

And that had to be the hardest nail he'd ever been given to chew on.

He promised not to use force, but he refused to stay out of sight. Greg would take Cougar along for the weekend, if only in his twisted mind.

Mark knew exactly what was going down. He stood at the front window until the bread truck showed up, and then he disappeared. Celia found him under his bed, but she could not reach him. On the verge of tears, she asked for Cougar's help. Bad assignment, but that was the kind he'd asked for.

"I'll go out and meet him," she said. "I don't want him coming to the door."

"C'mon, partner. We don't let our women go first. They follow us so they don't get…" *Shot.* "Well, they follow us. We're their shield. C'mon." The little hand slipped into his. It felt cold. As soon as he had the boy out from

under the bed, he rubbed the small hand between his two big ones and then slung the kid
on his back.

He tried to lighten up the moment a little.
The darker the moment, the better the time
for Indian humor. "Get behind us, woman.
Five paces."

The fact that she complied told him she
wasn't herself.

Banyon sat there in his bread truck, having
himself a smoke. Right there Celia had good
cause not to put her kid in the vehicle. He
was doing it just to show her he could. Cougar had to work hard to keep the flashes of
things *he* could do from taking control of his
hands. He put them under the soles of Mark's
tennis shoes like two stirrups to remind himself of his priority. *Support.*

And then, suddenly, he heard a third voice.

"Cougar, don't."

Words? So quiet, so small. *But words.*

Cougar paused and turned his head slightly until he could feel the boy's breath in his ear.

"Don't let him take me."

Oh, God. Oh, God, oh, God. Cougar reached across his own belly and patted the knobby little knee resting in the crook of his elbow.

"Does he have school next week?" Greg asked Celia as they approached the vehicle. He pretended not to notice Cougar walking in front of her. No surprise, he wasn't getting out of the van. He flicked his cigarette into Celia's driveway. "I'm supposed to have vacation time with him sometime this summer."

"You didn't schedule it," she said.

"I know. I wanna schedule it now."

The velvet noose tightened around Cougar's neck.

Banyon finally looked up and gave him the stink eye. "I haven't bothered you about that incident we had, but you have an anger management problem, buddy, and I have a complaint on file with the authorities."

"I'm not your buddy."

"Yeah, well, I've checked you out. You've got a little shell-shock thing goin', right? A little brain damage?" Stink eye turned smirky. "That's right, Sergeant. The rumors are flyin'." He leaned out the window just far enough to get a look at Celia.

Cougar imagined slamming his hand down on the back of Banyon's head and smashing his Adam's apple on the window ledge. The only thing stopping him was Mark.

"Did you know that about your war hero, Cecilia? They cracked his melon."

"Jesus," Cougar growled.

"I know him," Celia said. "And I know you, Greg. And this is not the time to discuss—"

"When?" Greg barked. "When would be a good time? Because I've got a few more things I intend to discuss. Like the terms of the custody agreement. You've got this guy living here, and he's got a hair-trigger temper. I've seen it for myself. It's a matter of police record."

"I won't let you do this, Greg."

"Put my son down. He's coming with me." He leaned sideways to take another shot at Celia. "And you'd better give a little more thought to signing those papers I brought you. You're about to hand me primary custody, and then maybe I won't need your signature."

Cougar gently loosened the human collar around his neck. "I gotta put you down, partner."

Mark buried his nose behind Cougar's ear. "Don't."

"You gotta say it out loud, Mark. You gotta tell him yourself."

"Cut the crap," Banyon spat. "He can't hear you, thank God, and he can't talk. And I'm gonna see that we get paid for that. We'll be set for life. He'll have nursing care, twenty-four seven. No worries. Right, son?"

"No," Mark said.

"What?" Banyon's eyes widened. He could've been some kind of a bug under a microscope.

He turned his damn bug eyes on Cougar. "What are you, a ventriloquist?"

Mark slipped his legs free and slid down Cougar's back. He stood steadily on his own two feet and repeated the word.

Bug eyes shifted to Celia. "How long has this been going on? They've got him talking, and you didn't say anything to me?"

"*They?* You mean the doctors?" Celia stepped forward and put her hands on the boy's shoulders. "Mark has himself talking for the first time. Not the first time *ever*— you don't even remember, do you, Greg— but the same first word. Clear as a bell." She glanced over her shoulder. She had a smile for her man. "Clear as a bell," she whispered.

"Can he hear, too?" Banyon looked down at the boy. "Can you hear me, Mark?"

"Staying here," Mark said.

"No, you're not." The Adam's apple Cougar had wanted to smash was bobbing up and down now like a happy frog. "I'm your father, and this is my weekend."

"I'm taking him to see his doctor, Greg." She took a step back. Mark moved with her. "You call your lawyer."

"You know what? I carry all my paperwork with me. I'll go to the cops. I'll show them the court order, and I'll be back with the law on my side." With a flat hand he banged the buns painted on the side of the bread truck. "I'll take him to the doctor myself. I wanna know what's goin' on here."

"Staying with Flyboy," Mark said.

"Now, that doesn't even make any sense. Baby talk. He's mentally impaired, just like..."

Banyon risked a finger by pointing it at Cougar. "Your friend here."

Cougar laughed. "You don't dare step out of that van, Banyon, and Mark says he's not getting in. Go find yourself a cop."

"Do you think he will?"

Celia lay beside Cougar on the bed they hadn't turned down in the clothes she hadn't taken off. His shoulder pillowed her head, and his shirt smelled of wood smoke and sage. She wanted to peel it off and make love to him even though it seemed like an unseemly wish after all that had happened. But he had made it happen, and it was all good, and she longed to draw him into her body and make it even better.

At least part of her did. But she had to put

that part on the back burner. Mark was asleep in the next room.

"Bring a cop? Not tonight." He pressed his lips to her forehead. "What I'm thinking about is you. You're a strong woman who's raising a warrior."

"A warrior?"

"Somebody who can stand his ground. You're doing it just right, Celia. He's coming. He's been a shooting star, chasing his own demons away. You know what that's like? He's coming back to you."

She smiled against the dark. "He's coming back to Flyboy."

"Yeah." He went quiet for a moment. Too quiet for her comfort. "And Flyboy should stay here. But I need to find myself another parking space."

She went numb. "You said you wouldn't let him run you off."

"It's not him. It's the law." He sighed. The night air was too heavy. It was clearly weighing him down. "Look, I don't know much about child custody, but I do know it's no good to take chances with kids' lives."

"I would never do that. Not…not intentionally."

"I didn't mean it that way, Celia. Stop beating yourself up. I don't understand why any court would ever side with that ass—" He drew a deep breath and blew it out like some kind of cleansing agent. "He's right about one thing. I have a history. I have a record of… I went off the deep end when I got out of the hospital and came back stateside. I got wasted for days at a time, got into fights, got hold of a pistol and I—" deep, dark, painful silence "—decided against using it."

"On yourself?"

"I wanted to check out. I was no good to anybody. I was on another planet, and the people around me looked at me like I was wired. I could explode anytime, and I knew what that looked like. I've seen it. It kills.

"So, my brother, Eddie—used to call him Eddie Machete because he can be tough when he has to be—anyway, my little brother checked me back in. And I'm doing pretty good. Even better since I met you. But you don't need me and my crazy past parked out in your yard."

"I need you right here, Cougar. In my home. In my bed." Her hand stirred over his powerful chest. "I need you in my life."

"You're on a roll with your life. Your son is on the mend. You're making a home here. You've got a good career going, good friends." He covered her hand with his. "I feel like I've just climbed out of a dark hole. I've got the sun in my face, thanks to you and Mark. I can feel the wind at my back. But I'm not sure what I'm gonna do now."

"Aren't you a warrior?"

She had some nerve asking a question like that, and she knew it. But it wouldn't do to coddle a warrior. He'd been telling her that all along. She waited for an answer.

It came in a soft chuckle, a quaking chest. "I'm a wounded warrior. Early retirement with a service-connected disability. Ever hear of a thirty-four-year-old retiree?"

"No. But I don't know too many decorated

wounded warriors, either. None, actually. But I'd like to meet a few more."

"Why?"

"Maybe do a little comparison shopping. I'd like to take you off the market, but if you're going to sell yourself short now that you've shown me your plethora of talents..."

"Plethora?"

"That's like the mother lode, Cougar, and I happen to be a single mother."

"Hmm. Plethora of talents." He was on the verge of a good comeback—she could feel it. "Name me five."

She laughed. "*You* name your five. And then I'll name you five more."

"First one that comes to mind is one I didn't know I had. I have a talent for loving."

"Don't start with a lie. You've never doubted that one."

"I didn't say making love. I said *loving*." He turned to her. "I'm loving you every minute of every day, Celia. I didn't know I had it in me."

She could hardly draw breath.

"You don't have to say it if you don't want to, but I wish you would."

She slammed her fist against his chest. "Then what's the deal with finding a different place to park your damn—"

"Why can't you say it? I know you're afraid of me, and you should, be, but I also know—"

"I love you." She pounded on him again. "Of course I love you. *Me* scared of *you?* You're the one who's ready to drive off into the sunset."

"Sunrise. I'm a red road kind of a guy." He held her fist close to his chest. "Please don't hit me again. You need as much muscle as you can get out of me, and believe me, I've got my weak spots." He lifted her hand to his lips. It was one of her favorite gestures of his. "Like I said, Celia, we can't take our chances with each other until we're sure I can't hurt Mark."

"There's no way."

"Greg thinks he has ways. He's got this lawsuit."

"It's *his* lawsuit. A thing like that—especially the way Greg's trying to work it—it could drag on for years. Mark's medical needs are already covered, and he has a nice little trust fund. And, Cougar, he can talk. He can *hear.*"

"I could maybe get a job as a tribal cop. If I can pass the background check, I've got the training."

"Is that something you want to do?"

"I haven't thought that far ahead. Not seriously. All I've been thinking about is how to be with you without adding to your problems."

"What problems?" She propped herself up on her elbow. "I have challenges. You have challenges. Mark has—"

"—challenges. I can handle all of it, Celia. All except one. Now that Mark's had a breakthrough, he's gonna tell us why he didn't wanna get into that bread truck. And if I have to choose between chewing nails and putting Mark in that truck…I'll be spitting nails in Banyon's face." He gave her a moment to digest that image. And then he offered quietly, "You think you could marry me?"

"Why wouldn't I be able to marry you?" He caught her upraised fist before she could do him any more harm. "Do you think you could come up with a better proposal? You're a decorated warrior, for heaven's sake. And you're obviously not retiring. You're moving on. So don't give me this—"

"Hey!" He uncurled her fingers and kissed her palm. "Will you take a Purple Heart as a down payment on a diamond ring?"

Her heart pounded inside its little cage. It wanted so much to take off and fly.

"I don't need a diamond," she whispered.

"I want to be the man you need. Not just part of him. All of him."

"Oh, Cougar, what I need is a true heart. I'll never know what you've been through—"

"I don't want you to."

"—but I know who you are. Mark knows you. Flyboy knows you. If you were to come up with a clear-cut, unambiguous proposal, then, yes, I think I'd be able to marry you." She laughed. "It would be worth it to watch you sign the license."

"You want my name?"

"I'm old-fashioned. I want your name."

"You'll get it, then. My wedding gift to you, my secret name." He put his hand on the back of her head and drew her to him for a kiss. "But trust me. It don't get any better than Cougar."

One week later, Cougar's outfit was still parked in Celia's yard. He still had his bed, and she still had hers. But that would all change soon. Maybe they were both a little old-fashioned, and that had its advantages. Anticipation was delicious. The big day would mark the beginning of beautiful nights spent in *their* bed and glorious sunrises viewed from their yard. Cougar was busy making his mark in both places—clear-cut, unambiguous and straight from a true heart. Maybe his head got a little screwed up sometimes, but he was working on some retraining. He and Mark were both on the red road.

He'd mounted Flyboy bareback and was working him on a hackamore when he saw Celia's little car top the rise on the highway. He dismounted quickly. He wanted to surprise Mark.

"What's the good word today, partner?" he asked as the two he awaited approached him.

"Flyboy."

The horse peered over the top fence rail, ears standing at attention.

Cougar chuckled. "If that horse could say a word, it would be Mark. How was your visit to the doctor?"

"Good." Mark's hand slid away from his mother's as he headed for the corral. "Flyboy!"

Cougar slipped his arm around Celia. "Any more good words?"

"Cougar." She offered her lips up to him for a kiss that ended in a smile. "And *brainpower*. Mark's brain has the power to turn itself around. The therapist says he wasn't refusing to talk or pretending not to hear. His

brain cut him off for some reason. Limited
his interaction with a world that kept poking
and prodding at him."

"He wants to take it slow. A step at a time,
a few words at a time. I know how that goes."
He walked her over to his pickup and opened
the passenger side door. "I have something
for you."

"A Purple Heart?"

"I couldn't even tell you where that is right
now. Let's see if I guess right." He took a
straw cowboy hat from a bag, put it on her,
adjusted the brim and grinned. "Perfect."

She took a look at herself in the pickup's
big side mirror. "You really think it's me?"

"I think it's a hat." He admired her reflec-
tion. "It looks great on you, and it'll protect
you a little bit. Wear it for me."

"Thank you." She kissed him again.

"I got one for Mark, too."

"He'll love it." She turned to lean back against the pickup door and folded her arms around herself. "I called Greg's lawyer and told him that I'm going to consult with another attorney. I told him that Mark's suddenly showing improvement, and all of a sudden there's a rush to accept the insurance company's offer. I'm pretty sure Mark's interests are not at the top of the list of concerns."

"You're a wise woman."

"Any money that comes out of this has to be put aside for Mark. Once Greg gets that through his head…"

"Yeah." He leaned back beside her and folded his arms. Two of a kind. "I know I won't miss him."

"I haven't heard anything from him this week. He said he was going to push for primary custody, and I'll be prepared for that battle."

"That's the one you can't take chances with."

"Well, I've been there, so I know the drill. Another court, another lawyer. As I said, I'm getting prepared."

"Look at that." Cougar nodded toward the corral, where Mark was nose to mustang nose between fence rails. "You'd think they were talking something over. According to *the book…*"

Celia flashed him a warning glance. "If you're sitting on a jealous streak, I might have to reconsider your proposal."

"Jealous of Logan Wolf Track? Not me."

He tipped his head back and smiled. "Okay, maybe a little envious of the book. Somebody writes a book, you gotta respect him for that."

"Respect is one of those good words."

"I'll give you plenty to respect me for. I've got a good head on my shoulders. You know, basically." He tugged at his hat brim. "I know, I know. I've got heart. You know, back in the day—I learned this from Dr. Choi, and I think it was the Civil War—PTSD was called *soldier's heart*. So that means I've got a soft heart. Not a good thing. See, we call it a warrior's heart. *Strong.*" He gestured with a fist. "I guess that's why I'd rather believe it's all in my head."

"There's nothing soft about your heart. Nothing soft about caring for people, putting others first."

"When I don't think too much, I get right in there and do what's necessary. Other times..." He looked into the eyes he was learning to trust beyond any he'd known. "Sometimes I'm scared, Celia. So scared I can hardly move. Trouble is, when the fear comes after the fact and the deed's already done..." He shook his head.

"That tells me a heart like yours is stronger than most. It holds on to who you really are, no matter what's going on around you." She slid his unbuttoned shirt aside and touched his chest. "You amaze me, Cougar. You've helped me understand my son."

"I wanted to hurt his father. Really, really bad."

"But you didn't." She glanced down at her hand. "You know what? Greg has never struck me physically. But emotionally… Well, he's never cared about me, either. Or Mark. It's all about Greg. It took me a while to realize how awful that is. It wasn't my fault. It wasn't me. It was *him*."

"You asked me about the program I was in, the one where we used horses…" He gave a self-deprecating chuckle. "The one where the horses were the ones giving the humans a leg-up. What are you thinking?" She questioned him with a look, and he touched her chin. "See, I'm getting to know you. I can tell you're thinking up some kind of a plan."

"Says the man who made plans to turn my deck into an entertainment center. You've been talking to Hank Night Horse, haven't you."

"Oh, now it's Night Horse." He winked at

her. "Who has my greatest respect. Actually, it was Sally. She wants me to take her to the VA hospital and show her around."

"Are you going to? Can Mark and I..." She turned toward the corral, and he followed her lead. Mark was inside the pen. With nothing but charisma he'd lured the mustang close to the fence, which he was about to use as a ladder. "Uh-oh."

"Can't keep a good man down," Cougar said as he pushed away from the pickup. "I'll take care of it."

Cougar eased his way into the corral through the gate and sidled up to Mark, who was determined to mount the horse. "Wait for me, partner. The three of us, we'll do this together." He rubbed Flyboy's shoulder with his left hand while he lifted Mark in his right arm. "If he says no, we back off. Okay?"

"Okay," Mark said. "Flyboy says okay."

"Put your arms over his back. Let him feel your belly against him." Mark followed instructions. The horse was relaxed. Cougar noticed Celia standing behind the gate. "Come join us," he told her quietly.

"I can ride now," Mark said.

Cougar lifted him onto the horse's back. He looked up and saw the face of a shooting star. He felt a warm hand slip into his, and he turned to find his woman, his wise and warm-hearted woman.

And the look in her eyes said, *It doesn't get any better than Cougar.*

* * * * *